SHADOW'S FLAME

SHADOW ISLAND SERIES: BOOK ELEVEN

MARY STONE
LORI RHODES

Copyright © 2023 by Mary Stone Publishing

All rights reserved.

No part of this book may be reproduced in any form or by any electronic or mechanical means, including information storage and retrieval systems, without written permission from the author, except for the use of brief quotations in a book review.

❦ Created with Vellum

For the valiant firefighters, whose bravery outshines the fiercest flames. This book is dedicated to you.

DESCRIPTION

Where there's smoke, there's murder.

As the sun dips toward the horizon at Dee's Dock, a yacht ignites more than just the evening sky— it sparks yet another deadly mystery on Shadow Island. Sheriff Rebecca West leads the charge as the tight-knit community bands together to battle the blaze. But as the smoke clears, a chilling discovery is made... arson is only the beginning, and the charred remains aboard signal murder.

Was the fire the ultimate goal, or was the blaze a smokescreen for a much darker deed?

Unfortunately, there are no witnesses to the crime. To make matters worse, the incident has triggered an FBI investigation into the increase in crimes on the island since Rebecca became sheriff.

Rebecca knows the spate of crimes is the result of her kicking the beehive of the previously untouchable Yacht

Club, and she suspects this case is no different. Of the three boats damaged by the fire, two belong to blue-collar business owners. The other belongs to a member of the Yacht Club.

The plot thickens when the leading suspect is found executed, forcing Rebecca and her team to sift through the ashes for answers. With every clue leading to more danger, they must catch a killer amidst the crosshairs of corruption before Shadow Island is consumed by the inferno of its own secrets.

From the tense beginning to the explosive conclusion, Shadow's Flame—the eleventh book in the Shadow Island Series by Mary Stone and Lori Rhodes—will draw you in like a moth to a flame. Just don't get burned.

1

It was so good to be back.

Dropping his bag, Bolivar MacDaniel waved as the charter boat he'd been working on pulled away from the dock where it had dropped him. The rest of the crew would be heading for the mainland, letting the others off closer to Norfolk.

Mac had only been gone for a week this time, which was a bit shorter than most of his fishing gigs. Even so, it was always a relief to set his feet on land again.

Luck had been with them, and their fishing trip had wrapped up a day earlier than planned when the coolers filled with tuna. All he needed to do now was haul his gear to his car and drive home. His wife wasn't expecting him for at least another day, so this would be a fun surprise.

Mac glanced toward the horizon, where the sun was just beginning its descent into the sea. There were about two hours of daylight left. If he didn't waste time, he could still make it for a sunset walk with Paula. They didn't get a lot of nights together, so they both treasured the time they did have. Watching the sun fall below the horizon, the sky shifting from amber to blue, the air cooling on their cheeks...nothing was more romantic than an evening stroll.

He scanned up and down the stretch of coastline. Deserted. Everyone was probably having dinner with their loved ones. Soon enough, that would be him too.

Unfortunately, he'd packed too fast upon learning they'd be returning ahead of schedule and had to dig through his bag to find his car keys. He chuckled to himself, thinking about how Paula would curse nonstop as she searched her purse for keys that she swore had to be hidden at the bottom.

Taking inspiration from his wife, he shoved his hand to the bottom of his jam-packed duffel, which required him to kneel and put his arm in all the way up to his shoulder. Wriggling his fingers, he was rewarded by the curve of a metal key ring and wrapped his fingers around it. The keys snagged repeatedly as he pulled, but with a bit of tugging, he managed to free them.

Time to go home.

Keys clenched in his teeth, he folded and secured the top of his bag. Now all he had to do was lug his equipment down the long pier at Dee's Dock and then up the gentle slope to where he'd left his car.

Mac stood, slinging the bag over his shoulder, and headed that way. He was already daydreaming about the kind of greeting his wife would give him when he arrived home.

Then he smelled the smoke.

Whirling around, he surveyed the boats lining both sides of the dock. Working crafts of all kinds crowded the dock, front to back. There was even an extra vessel he could barely perceive beyond a row of others on his left.

Could someone be grilling on their ship? Though not

uncommon, the smell was wrong. This wasn't the scent of meat cooking.

Mac took several steps, looking for the source of the scent. He only made it a few feet before a thin stream of smoke rose over the boats. Dropping his bag, he shoved his keys into his pocket and ran.

Smoke billowed from a cabin on a boat two slips closer to the shore. A light was on inside it. Whether it was from the flames or a bulb, he wasn't sure.

"Hey! You okay in there?"

When no one answered, Mac climbed aboard. It was a fishing vessel with an awning that covered half the back deck. His gaze landed on that boat he'd noticed a minute ago. It was a large yacht with an angled canopy.

That's odd. Why would a yacht be here?

This dock was for deepwater working boats. All the yachts were moored elsewhere.

Rushing under the awning, he spotted the stairs that led down to the cabins and another set that led up to the steering. The smell of gasoline hit him, and he pulled his phone from his pocket to call 911.

"Ahoy, the boat!" He cupped his free hand to his mouth in an effort to be heard. "Anyone down there? Can you hear me?"

The crackle of flames was his only response.

Shit. Shit. Shit. I need a damn fire extinguisher. Now.

He looked around, searching for one. The fire belowdecks wasn't big yet. If he could put it out, he could save precious minutes before help arrived.

Tapping on his phone's keypad, he headed back to the dock. He'd search another boat for an extinguisher while he called the fire department.

He'd just tapped *nine* when a searing pain detonated at

the back of his head. His world exploded into a cacophony of dazzling lights. He teetered sideways and reached out for something—anything—that could anchor him to reality. The cruel void met his desperate search, offering no solace or stability.

Finding nothing but air, Mac was hurled into the abyss.

What the hell?

Had it been a minute? An hour? Disoriented by space and time, Mac groaned.

Pain stabbed through his skull the instant he tried to roll over. His head pounded like he'd just finished a three-day bender, but that didn't add up. Forcing his eyelids apart, he saw light pulsing and dancing around the small cabin. He slammed his eyes shut again.

Heat. It's so hot. What's going on?

He struggled to gather his scattered thoughts. He was lying on something hard, harder than even his bunk. Rolling to his side, away from the heat, he gasped. Pain crackled in his head. Taking a deep breath, he coughed. The smell finally registered, and he opened his eyes in horror.

Smoke filled the room. Thick and darkened from the burning area rugs and varnished wood. Flames leaped into view.

There was no air, and he barely managed to croak out one word. "Help."

On his hands and knees, he tried to escape the heat from the fire. Black smoke engulfed his body, even low to the floor as he was. Memories flickered as the flames encroached.

He'd been on the dock. Was about to go home to

surprise his wife. A sunset walk. Then he'd seen the smoke on a boat. He'd rushed onto the boat and then...what?

He tried to make out his surroundings. There was the metal leg of a table and the base of a curved bench. This was the galley. Somehow, he'd fallen down the stairs and wound up here, where the fire had started.

If he wanted any chance of survival, he had to get out. Bracing his hands on the bench, he pushed himself to his feet. His head spun as his balance shifted. After spending most of his life on ships, his sea legs were rock steady, yet he couldn't keep his footing.

Years of working on chartered fishing excursions told him he had a limited amount of time to get off the boat under these conditions. If he stayed there much longer, the fire would spread to the fuel tanks, and he'd be blown right out of the water.

He clenched his eyes tight against the pain throbbing in his head. It felt like any moment his eyes would explode from the pressure behind them. He held his arm up in front of his face, trying to stave off the smoke.

There was nothing but heat. Lunging forward, he prayed he'd find the stairs leading up to fresh air and safety. Fire raced over the surface of the counter next to him. He jerked away from it, slamming his hip into something he could not see.

His throat burned, and he started coughing. It was like a furnace in his chest as the fire cascaded down the cupboards and approached his feet. Mac shuffled forward, not sure if he was walking toward or away from the exit. All he knew was that he had to move.

A jarring *boom* resounded overhead. The concussion of it knocked him forward, forcing him back onto his hands and knees.

Air. He needed air.

It was so hard to breathe. He couldn't stop coughing. Swiping a hand across his eyes, he tried to clear his vision. He could barely make out what was in front of him.

A metal square with a handle that ran along the top. An oven.

The galley.

In his desperation, he must've stumbled deeper into the galley instead of toward the stairs. Flames crept down around him as the fiberglass ceiling above melted.

Mac opened his mouth to scream for help once again. He never even heard the second boom as the propane tank for the stove exploded in the heat.

2

"Crap."

Sheriff Rebecca West stood beside the open door of her cruiser where she'd just parked next to the dock house at Dee's Dock.

The sun was about an hour away from leaving them in twilight. Shadows stretched long, distorted by the dance of flames racing along the dock, the boats, and even across the water itself. Heavy black smoke billowed from the entire right side of the wooden walkway, obscuring her view. She tried to make sense of what she was seeing to formulate the best plan.

Viviane was right. This was bad, and even from her vantage point, Rebecca could see that it could easily get much worse.

Up and down the dock, people disappeared and reappeared through the smoke, calling out to each other as they ran. Their words were jumbled from the crackling roar of fire and the slap of waves.

High tide was about three hours away, so they had

limited time before the waves would push the burning watercraft to shore.

Was that good or bad? Rebecca didn't know.

Slamming her door shut, she darted around the raised porch of the dock house and down the ramp to join the swarm. Once she was below the belching smoke, she watched people of all ages running with buckets, axes, knives, and hoses. The boats that weren't engulfed in flames had been cut loose and pushed out of harm's way by anyone who could reach them.

A fire brigade had started, with good Samaritans lining the edge of the dock where it was safe from the heat. They pulled up seawater, passing buckets over their heads to the waiting hands of the next person. Two pitiful hoses worked along the pier, but they didn't seem to make any difference to the blue-white flames.

The roar of a heavy engine caught Rebecca's attention. She was surprised she could hear anything over the shouting and the devouring noises of the fire. A silvery red fireboat raced in from the north, coming around the curve of the island.

Before it even seemed close enough to help, it shot a large stream of water from below its hull. As the boat neared, the driver skillfully maneuvered the water cannon, targeting the fiercest patches of the blaze with impressive precision.

With a cacophony of curse words and prayers, the bucket brigade dropped what they were doing and ran to the ramp that led them back to shore, away from the drenching spray. Rebecca stepped aside as they passed before turning to watch the firefighters work. All of them were dressed in casual clothing. Volunteers who'd dropped everything to run out and help when needed.

"Sheriff!"

Rebecca turned to find Deputy Greg Abner on the porch of the dock house. His silver hair served as a stark contrast to his deep tan, acquired from countless hours on his fishing boat. He'd come out of retirement to help her get the two new deputies trained.

Right beside him was one of the new ones, Jake Coffey, a Virginia State Trooper until recently. Even at a distance, his piercing blue eyes stood out against the evening sky. Her newest deputy had come highly recommended by VSP Special Agent Rhonda Lettinger. The two men ran down the ramp.

"Where do you want us, Sheriff?" Jake was slightly out of breath as he paused next to her—not from any lack of fitness, but because the air was getting harder to breathe.

The fire on the dock was almost out, and ropes of smoke swirled through the heated air as the cool ocean water from the fireboat arched over it. Nowhere on the docks was safe now, as structural integrity had been compromised by the fire. Cool mist and superheated air washed over them in waves, revealing charred areas.

Rebecca turned and motioned for them to retreat. It would only get worse once the firefighters turned their attention to the boats.

They reached the porch, where they could talk without having to scream. The civilians who'd run over to assist earlier were spreading out, walking through the tall grasses on the shore. None of them paid any attention to the police among them. Everyone's focus was centered on the fire.

Greg tapped Jake's shoulder. "See that guy in the white shirt with the red axe?" Jake nodded. "That's Dee Newton. He's the owner of the dock and head of the fire crew as well. Coordinate with him."

As Jake ran off, Rebecca raised her pen camera toward one group of people.

She caught Greg staring. "Just in case. I'm going to take a quick video. Firebugs like hanging around to watch their fires but leave as it gets extinguished."

"Which means you need to make sure you get the shots while the fire is still burning." He kept his gaze locked on the water, but she still heard the hint of condemnation in his voice because she wasn't rushing forward to put out the fires. It stung a little, but she tried to shrug it off.

Rebecca nodded, pivoting so she got the entire scene in detail. "Truthfully, there are enough people helping with fire control already. I'd rather document evidence."

Greg grunted as she finished and tucked the camera into her pocket. "That makes sense." He gestured at the people who were sliding down the hill toward the water. Jake was already down there, up to his waist as he pulled a tired swimmer in. "They're going to be cold as hell. Follow me inside. I know where the blankets are kept."

"On the right in the blue bins." Rebecca walked beside him.

He slid his eyes over to her. "You been here before?"

"I wasn't just standing there twiddling my thumbs before you showed up. Situations like this, where I'm one of the last on the scene and everyone seems to know what they're doing, it's best to hang back and take it all in first. I heard Dee telling people to come in and get blankets."

Rebecca yanked open the door to the dock house. It was weather-beaten and smaller inside than it looked. The land side of the building was for parts and repairs. There was a wall with a doorway dividing it down the middle. The side she was on was for the dock renters. It was a basic reception area with two metal-and-plastic chairs along the front wall and a counter that served as the room divider.

Wooden racks holding brochures flanked an old corkboard slathered in business cards and help-wanted flyers. Under that was a stack of four long blue tubs. Rebecca popped the lid on the top one. It was filled to capacity with carefully folded woolen blankets.

"Good thinking, Sheriff."

Rebecca turned to find that a man carrying a fire axe had followed them in. He was the same one Greg had pointed out as Dee.

"Haul those down and get as many people wrapped as you can. Couple of folks got their arms and legs burned when the fire flared up. It's not cold, but the water's a bit chilly. That, plus the shock will get to them. We got ambulances on the way?"

Greg pulled out his radio. "Dispatch, what's the ETA on those buses?"

"The vans from the health center should be there any minute, but they don't have sirens. Keep an eye out for them. The ambulances have just crossed the bridge. Another five minutes they said, since you're on the opposite side of the island."

Even though he was new to his position, Elliot Ping was already settling into his job as dispatcher and didn't sound as shaky as he had even a week ago.

Rebecca checked the second blue tub and found that it, too, was filled with blankets.

Dee was busy moving around behind the counter. "Greg, come help me with this. The sheriff looks like she can handle the blankets. But we need to get something warm in their bellies too."

The aroma of coffee took over the small space in no time as the two men gathered Styrofoam cups and two carafes.

"I'll meet you outside, gentlemen. Greg, while you're handing that out, see if you can get some answers about what happened."

Rebecca stacked the tubs on top of each other and hoisted them up, barely able to peer over the top bin. They were heavier than she'd expected, but she managed to push open the door with her back. She was grateful the pain from her previous injuries was gone and no longer impacted her ability to help the great people of Shadow Island.

Two dozen souls, some visibly scarred from burns, others shivering uncontrollably, gathered in the aftermath. Rebecca hated that the thin comfort of blankets and the warmth of hot coffee were all they had to stave off their immediate suffering. Thankfully, medical assistance would arrive shortly.

As Rebecca looked over the huddled figures, she sent a silent plea skyward, hoping against hope that everyone would pull through.

3

Luck, along with the quick actions of Dee's volunteer fire crew, had contained the flames to three boats and a section of the dock. Four people were being treated for smoke inhalation. Two more had burns serious enough to need treatment at the health center. But no one was hurt so badly they needed to be taken to the hospital in Coastal Ridge. Considering the height of the flames when Rebecca arrived, that was a miracle.

"Why is the water still on fire?" Rebecca had thought she was talking to herself and was surprised when she got a response from a familiar voice.

"It's probably the engine oil that spilled out during the fire. Or enough gasoline mixed with the water to make it flammable." Viviane walked up next to her. She was wearing a tank top and a loose, flowy skirt, though the fabric had been pulled up, tucked between her legs, and tied around her waist. "It won't go out 'til the firefighters can cool it enough by spraying a mist of water over it. Either that or the misting will choke it out."

Rebecca glanced out at the water where the fireboat was

moving around the last burning circle. She turned back to Viviane, smiling at her friend's odd fashion choice. "That makes sense. I guess."

Viviane caught her staring and grinned, kicking her right leg out. "What? Have you never seen someone gird their loins before?" She giggled and turned a wide-legged circle, showing off. "I wasn't going to waste time changing when Mama said there was a fire at the docks, so I girded up before hitting the pier. Long skirts and fire are a bad combination."

As always, it made sense when Viviane explained it, but Rebecca was continuously surprised at how unencumbered her way of thinking was. Then she smiled more broadly as she realized it wasn't all that different from her own. Viviane was an expert at finding new ways around problems. Rebecca hated being stonewalled, so she always looked for a work-around.

"Anyway, I just wanted to check on you and make sure you were good. They're making a fresh pot of coffee for anyone who wants it." Viviane pointed up the gentle slope of the beach. "We're all getting caffeinated before we need to start hauling the boats in."

Dee and Greg were still passing out hot drinks, checking on the people trying to warm up and dry off as the last warm rays of the day faded from the sky. Most of the civilians who'd been running the bucket brigade were gathered near the building.

Volunteer firefighters had shown up right after Rebecca. Their crew was tentatively walking the dock, checking every char mark and jabbing the wood with their axes to check the integrity of the structure. They'd set up floodlights to make the task easier on everyone.

The boats that had escaped the fire were bobbing on the

waves, anchored safely out of the way. The three boats that had burned were ready to be pulled to shore.

"We need to figure out what happened here. Have you seen the fire marshal?" Rebecca debated getting a fresh cup of coffee. Her throat was dry and raw from the smoke and having to yell.

She noticed Jake was wrapped in a blanket as well. It looked like a bulky shawl with his blue eyes peeking out from the rough fabric. He'd been in the water, loading up buckets for the fire brigade.

Viviane nodded toward a short man with a bald head and clean-shaven face near the parking lot. The upper section of his navy blue extrication suit was unzipped and hanging around his waist. Wide reflective strips wrapped around both upper sleeves, flashing in the failing light.

"He's right there, the super shiny guy. Gil Bentley. Showed up a bit ago but has been on his radio the whole time. I think he's coordinating with the guys on the boat."

Fire marshals in this area didn't normally ride out with the firefighters. They were the investigators who got to work once the fire was out. Until then, it was the fire chiefs who had control of the scene.

It was the same reason that Rebecca and her people were only permitted to assist. Fire was not something she had jurisdiction over. Not until the fire marshal said so. And he didn't have jurisdiction until the fire was safely out.

Deciding the coffee would be put to better use by the people still trying to warm up, Rebecca thanked Viviane and headed over to talk to the marshal.

As she approached, his eyes ran over her, top to bottom, then back up again. He gave the barest upward flick of his chin in greeting. "Sheriff."

"Marshal." Rebecca returned his nod.

"I'm Gil Bentley. And your name?"

"Rebecca West. Anything my crew and I can do to help? We'd like to know if this was a criminal act or accidental. If it's anything criminal, we need to start gathering evidence."

"That's why I'm here. I've already talked with sea patrol. The boats are too burned to be seaworthy. We need to get them beached before they can be searched." He shook his head. "And you're not going to be much help. Not unless you've got gloves." Without looking, he gestured to the coil of rope that had been dropped in the sand by one of the divers.

Rebecca grimaced, remembering the last time she'd had to haul on a rope. It had been to save a man stuck on his roof in the beginning stages of a hurricane. The nylon had left rope burn and painful splinters in her palms, and she'd spent the rest of that day with swollen, aching hands wrapped in bandages. And that had been after getting the splinters cut out of her flesh by Darian Hudson.

Her heart squeezed at the thought of her fallen deputy, and she had to force her mind back to the present.

"I've got a pair in the cruiser. We'll be right back." She gestured toward Greg and Jake. "Come on, gents. It's time to bring this in."

It was only six more steps to her cruiser. But by the time she'd gotten her gloves from the door cubby and pulled them on, the remaining volunteers and law enforcement were halfway down the slope. Cold, wet, tired, sore, bruised, and still lining up to help one more time.

Rebecca tromped down the trail along with them. Men and women tossed off their blankets, some using them to protect their hands from the rope. A woman she didn't know glanced up, smiled, and gestured at a spot in the hauling line, waiting for her to join them. They had to crowd together, which meant working in unison and pulling hand over hand while standing shoulder to shoulder.

This is home.

It was less a thought and more of a feeling. The sense that she fit in. Rebecca took her place with the rest of the people working to make their island safer. As she pulled, she remembered the open comradery she'd been a part of while working on the sandbag line before the hurricane. Looking around, these could be the same people now as then. Even if they weren't, this was the same feeling.

"Nice and smooth, folks. Nice and smooth." Bentley stood at the front of the rope, his heavy rubber boots in the water. All his focus was centered on the charred hull, topped with a scorched metal frame and fiberglass so melted, it looked like a Salvador Dalí painting.

Hand over hand, they towed the boat in. It was easy enough while it was in the water, and the incoming high tide helped. Water had protected the lower half of the boat, leaving it unblemished and easy to steer. But getting the hull dragged up onto the shore was another story. The keel dug into the sand before the marshal called a halt.

"The name is still half legible, *Shoreline Catch*. Let me get a look inside before we do anything else. I don't want to crack this open by accident." Bentley gestured for some of the firefighter crew who'd finished walking the dock to come join the effort.

To make room for the newcomers, the civilians backed off and climbed the slope to the parking lot. The fire marshal pulled a flashlight from one of his breast pockets.

Two of the approaching firefighters, both tall and blond, similar enough to be brothers, stepped forward and squatted down. They held their hands in front, giving the marshal a boost up to see over the fiberglass that drooped over the gunwale.

The flashlight clicked on, and Bentley moved the beam back and forth. It was too high for Rebecca to see what he was looking at. She backed up the hill, both to get out of their way and to try and get a look inside the ship.

Bentley stiffened so abruptly, he nearly toppled backward. "Yeah, Sheriff, this one is going to involve you and your crew. The deck burned away, and the bottom is full of water. We've got a floater in here."

"A body? In the boat?"

Shit. Shit. Shit.

Rebecca turned away from the boat containing the corpse, searching for Dee. He was part of the crowd and easy enough to spot with his jaw hanging open in horror. When he caught her eyes, he shook his head in denial.

Behind him, the vans from the medical center had just parked. Paramedics began to work their way through the crowd, triaging patients.

"We acted as fast as we could." Dee shifted, moving to stare at every person.

Most had helped themselves to blankets to protect them from the cool night breeze now that they weren't active. Others had pulled on jackets or hoodies, but nearly every face was obscured in the growing twilight as they huddled together talking.

Watching Dee, Rebecca realized that he was taking a head count in an attempt to figure out who had died.

"We all worked as fast and as best as we could, Dee. You and your crew were fighting the blaze before the firefighters even got here. Now I need you to find the registration for the boats that burned." Rebecca pointed to the charred section of the docks.

Dee didn't seem to track the movement as he stared into the middle distance.

Viviane moved up next to him and wrapped her arm around his shoulders. A short, dark-haired man clapped him on the back, leaning in to speak to him.

Whatever he said snapped Dee out of his shock, and he started nodding. "Yeah. Registration. Yeah. I can do that. But only for two. That one, the yacht, wasn't registered here. The cheap bastard didn't pay for berthing or even talk to me about it. But if that's the *Shoreline*, then the other boat is most likely the *Look Around*."

"It was anchored, not docked." One of the women getting her arm wrapped used her good hand to wave at the yacht still sitting in the water. "The yacht, I mean. I'm Bethany Wriggle. Good to meet you, Sheriff."

"Then how did it catch on fire?"

Rebecca didn't see who among the crowd asked that, but it was a damn good question. One that she sadly did not have the ability to answer. For that, she'd have to rely on the fire marshal.

"I know everyone here is tired, probably cold, and wants to go home. But I'm going to need you all to hold on just a bit longer. Deputies Coffey and Abner and I are going to need to take your statements."

"I'll need those as well." The fire marshal walked up to join them. "We're not going to be hauling in any of the other boats. I've got towboats on the way to move them to a launch to load onto trailers. We're going to take all three in for evidence."

"What about the body?" Rebecca's shoulders tensed with anxiety at the idea of her crime scene being disturbed like that.

Bentley's eyes narrowed, surveying the area. "M.E. is on

the way. I'll coordinate with her how to move forward. But I'm not going to risk any lives trying to search those vessels. If we go climbing in any of them now, we could sink along with all the evidence. I can let you know if we find any more victims on the other boats. State police boats are on the way too. They're bringing out divers in case anything fell into the water."

She was pretty sure he wouldn't want her arguing with him. It was stupid to try anyway. He was right, and she knew it.

Rebecca stepped closer so she couldn't be overheard. "Fire Marshal Bentley, is there any chance there's someone still alive in the boats? Someone we could save if they weren't moved first."

"There is." His voice was as low as hers, both of them aware of civilian ears all around them. "There could be innocent victims, and arsonists are often caught in their own fires. And from everything I've heard, this one spread freakishly fast, even for a boat fire. I've no way of knowing right now. That's why we need the boats from the state police to get here as soon as possible. Once they're made secure, we'll search through them, bow to stern."

Rebecca's gaze was drawn to the yacht bobbing in the waves. What she suspected was fiberglass fluttered in the wind. She couldn't tell what it was hung up on. Maybe an antenna of some kind. But it was eerie as all hell. Especially now that she knew its entire crew could be dead. Or worse, someone could be wounded and trapped.

Or dying as she stood here doing nothing.

4

Bethany Wriggle fidgeted as Rebecca took her statement, though Rebecca couldn't blame the poor woman. Nurse Missy was finishing dressing Bethany's burned arm, and it had to hurt.

"No. I didn't see the yacht come in. But I got in late last night, slept in, and didn't plan to come down 'til the tide was going out this evening. Then I got the call about the fire and hauled ass down here. I live just across the street."

Wriggle had been one of the first to hit the docks. According to her, if she'd been just a bit faster, they could have put it out before it spread to the dock and other boats.

Jake and Greg were talking to two men, both with burns on their arms and legs. They'd only made it through a handful of the people who'd come out to help with the blaze, focusing on those who needed to leave first. None of them had seen what started the fire. Most weren't even sure when it had started.

The boats that docked there were all deepwater commercial vessels. All the registered ones were accounted for. Two others were out on runs, and the rest had been tied up for the night. And since no one lived on the boats, no one had been around to see what happened.

"When did you first notice the yacht?" This story was going the same way as all the others had.

Wriggle shook her head. "Not 'til I saw it burning in the water. Before that, I was focused on the dock fire."

"And did you notice anyone else on the docks?"

Rebecca wasn't surprised when Wriggle shook her head. No one had seen anything. They rarely did. It was the story of law enforcement. Even when witnesses offered no valuable insight, they still expected the police to have all the answers.

Resisting the urge to merely mumble her thanks, Rebecca smiled warmly before turning to look for the next person in the interview queue. Everyone who'd given their statements had left for the health center already.

A tall, thin figure wearing a purple hoodie was heading toward the parking lot. Rebecca glanced over to make sure she hadn't missed anything. Both deputies were in the middle of taking statements.

When Rebecca turned back, the figure was nearly out of sight, but she caught up in no time. "Excuse me, we need everyone to give statements before leaving." Her words had no effect. Maybe it was because her voice was still strained from the smoke. Or maybe it was because the person didn't want to hear her. She tried again, louder this time. "Hey, you in the parking lot. I need to speak to you. Come back."

That time her shouting was acknowledged. Sort of. The person in the purple hoodie started running.

"Dammit!" Rebecca took off after them, her focus locked on the fleeing form. Most witnesses didn't run. Not unless they were trying to get away with something.

The parking lot lights had already come on, so Rebecca

easily made out the direction of the sprinter down the road. Gripping her radio, she called in her location. "Dispatch, pursuing witness fleeing on foot, Bayview Road heading north."

"Sheriff, state police are en route. ETA two minutes."

Talking while running wasn't easy, especially when the person she was chasing was running so fast. Bayview was one of the main roads in Shadow, nice, wide, and smooth. The steady pounding of her heart thrummed in her ears. She squeezed her radio again. "Send them to me."

Rebecca let go of the radio and focused on running faster. Ahead of her, the shape showed up in the next circle of light on the road. If she'd had the breath, she'd have cursed again. Whoever it was, they had covered impressive ground in mere moments.

They were getting away.

Hoyt's house was nearby, and for a moment, Rebecca debated calling him. He could be there in his truck in less than a minute.

The second slap of shoes on pavement stopped. Only Rebecca's echoed now.

Shit!

Decision time. To the left of the road was a residential area and the waterway, surrounded by soft terrain. To the right of the road, the side the figure had been running on, was a small business district. As she ran, Rebecca replayed every sound she'd heard.

There'd been no change of pace, nothing to indicate the runner had crossed the road. She hadn't heard any splashing or squelching of mud. As fast as they were moving, they'd have sunk if they'd headed into the mud lands.

Following her gut, Rebecca veered right, pulling her

flashlight from her belt and clicking it on as she raised it to her shoulder.

Bingo. There, in the dim glow, was a faint smudge of dark purple almost camouflaged by the night's shadows. The hoodie was likely cotton since nothing reflected in the beam of her light. Rebecca took a deep breath and pressed on.

"Stop! Sheriff! Stop running!"

The shape ahead of her stumbled, twisting around. For just a moment, Rebecca caught the smallest glimpse of the face under the hood. Just the forehead, but enough to realize she was chasing a tanned white person or a pale person of color.

Rebecca activated her radio. "All units. Light brown-skinned suspect, royal purple hoodie, dark-blue jeans, wearing sneakers, not sure of age or gender, about five-six or five-seven. Headed northwest."

This person might be fast on the road, but Rebecca was catching up now that they were on grass. There was a *squeak*, barely audible above the gentle wind. Rebecca had fallen enough while trekking through the marshes to know exactly what that sound was. Sneakers sliding on wet grass and reeds. The person had fallen.

Another clue. If she could just catch up by the time they hit the other side of the alley, she felt certain she would know who she was chasing.

Recovering from the stumble, they pushed to their feet again, silhouetted by the lights of the businesses they were running toward. As she ran, Rebecca couldn't help but think she knew the person ahead of her. She didn't even know if she was chasing a man or a woman. Still, once the feeling of familiarity had surfaced, she couldn't shake it.

Just a few more yards. Rebecca tried to put on another

burst of speed, but she was already running as fast as she could. The ground firmed up under her feet as the wet slap of shoes resounded off pavement once again. She was so close, less than ten feet away now.

Rebecca slipped and her knee landed in fresh mud. She'd stumbled in the same spot the runner had. The ground was torn up, making it even slicker. Rebecca's hands dropped reflexively, catching her weight, and she bounced up to continue the pursuit.

The footsteps grew fainter with every second. *Dammit.* Rebecca raced between the buildings. Her hand dropped to her gun. Coming out of a narrow corridor, she would be vulnerable to ambush.

Rebecca weighed the best course of action. Stopping and inching around the blind spot was one idea. Going wide to see around the corners wasn't a possibility, since the ambush could come from either side. She could tuck and roll, except she really didn't want to take another blow to her healing shoulder. That left her with one option.

She slowed, dropping low. Her heart pounded in her ears. As she reached the end of the alley, she darted to the left. All around her, the roads were empty in the business area she'd entered. Most of the shops were closed, either for the night or the season.

Rebecca spun in a circle, realizing she no longer heard the fleeing footsteps. Her gaze swept the area, jumping from light to dark and back to light.

Bright headlights flashed over her, followed by an even brighter beam. Rebecca jerked her hand up, trying to protect her eyes.

"State police, hold it right there."

She sighed. "Sheriff West. I lost the person I was chasing." Squinting hard, she lowered her hand to point at the badge on her belt. "I couldn't tell if they were armed, but they were fast. They're wanted for questioning involving a case of arson that ended with a death."

The searchlight moved to track along the road.

"There!" Rebecca pointed at the single muddy footprint on the sidewalk, then followed it to the next one on the road.

One of the troopers spilled out of the passenger door. "There's another cruiser right behind us."

"Good. Start searching." Rebecca crossed the street, trailing additional footprints, until the mud wore off just before an intersection. She ran down the sidewalk, the trooper behind her as the cruiser pulled ahead to the end of the block. The spotlight swept back and forth, searching.

There were no sounds, no tracks, nothing to follow.

Rebecca grabbed the radio. "Abner, I lost the runner. Ask the people still there if they know who was wearing the purple hoodie. I'll be back as soon as I can."

It wasn't a cold night. From the little she'd seen, the person she'd been tracking hadn't been wet either. Which invited the question, why were they wearing a hoodie? They could be hiding burns. Or blood.

A pit settled in her stomach as she realized she might have just let the killer slip away.

5

Rebecca hitched a ride back to the dock. With the lights from the boats working just off the shore, coupled with the floodlights the volunteer firefighters had posted, the strip of beach was lit up like midday. The scent of fire lingered in the still night air. The few onlookers had moved to higher ground as the high tide continued to encroach on the shore.

Fewer cars were in the parking lot now than when she'd run through it. Both medical vans and the two ambulances had already left. The group of witnesses was much smaller as well. Dee had pulled a blanket from a tub before converting the tub into a makeshift bench.

With no more people for him to help, he was finally taking care of himself. His eyes were red, which could be from quietly crying or the sting of smoke and fumes. Either way, Rebecca couldn't do much to help except give him an understanding smile and nod as she walked past.

"What do you have, Coffey?"

Her newest deputy twisted to look at her and held up a Styrofoam cup. "Coffee, of course. Little birdie told me you like yours with lots of cream, one sugar, and often." Jake was catching on fast, not that she'd expected much of a learning curve for the state police transfer.

Rebecca smiled. Fresh cups of coffee after a run had that effect on her. "Hopefully, you have some information for me too. Were you able to get the registration info on the boats?"

"All three of them. We've got the *Shoreline Catch*, owned by a local named Cole Fairbank. He conducts fishing tours, and according to the rest of the people we talked to, he was also known to bring in his own catch to sell a time or two."

"Not unusual around here. People need a job that will either carry them through the offseason or is flexible enough to do something else during the downtime." Rebecca pointed toward the boat still sitting on the shore. "Is that the one?"

"That's the one." Jake indicated the well-lit boat in the water, surrounded by tugboats. "And that's the *Look Around*. You might have guessed from the name that it's a tour boat that specializes in whale watching during the fall and winter, plus bay- and shore-sightseeing trips for the rest of the year."

"Who owns the *Look Around*?"

Jake checked his notepad. "That would be Perry Ballard. He's another local. Owns Shadow Boat Tours. According to Jenna Dean, a lovely and talkative middle-aged woman, he's also mid-forties with thinning hair and brown eyes, and has a real looker of a wife."

"And the third one?"

"The last one was easy. Its name was still intact. *Liquid Asset*. Who the hell names a boat something like that?"

That name sounded familiar. Rebecca sipped her coffee, trying to find the answer in caffeine. The connection floated up in her mind. "I saw that name at the Seaview Marina.

The owner is part of the Yacht Club. I'm fairly certain it belongs to Oswald Chapman." Rebecca rubbed her fingers over her stinging eyes. "I already know that's going to lead us someplace complicated. Let's start with the other two."

Jake raised an eyebrow, cocking his head to the side. "You're the boss."

"You learn 'boss' from the others?"

He smiled but didn't answer her directly as he tucked his notes away in his pocket. "Two blue-collar guys and an Aqua Mafioso. Which one of these things don't belong?"

"We don't have any mobster yet. Or Yacht Club member. Only the yacht. It could've been stolen or driven down for reasons we don't yet know. We need to find out why it's anchored here instead of the marina."

A set of headlights swinging into the parking lot caught Rebecca's attention. It was most likely another state police cruiser. She was still waiting for a response from the troopers who'd gone to find her runner.

"I'll check to see if anyone's reported it stolen. If not, I'll find out why it's here and when it showed up."

Rebecca queued her radio. "Abner, can you make a quick swing through the Seaview Marina parking lot?"

The answer was immediate. "Roger that. Am I looking for anything specific?"

"The usual. Blood splatters. Damaged property. Mayhem. Screams." Jake's eyebrows shot up at her answers. "Or any signs of theft. We've got one of their burned boats down here."

Laughter was the first response. "It's a Thursday night. I'd expect nothing else from those stuck up—" The channel went dead before his last words came through. Greg was a bit old-fashioned. He didn't like using harsh language in front of Rebecca. She thought it was stinking adorable.

She was about to respond in kind until she noticed who was walking from the parking lot. "This is a lucky break already, and we just started our investigation. Rhonda, what are you doing out here?"

Special Agent Rhonda Lettinger of the Bureau of Criminal Investigations within the Virginia State Police marched toward them, nodding a terse greeting to Jake but addressing Rebecca. "When you call out half our boats and six of our cruisers, that tends to shake people up. And those people call me and make me come down too." She sighed heavily. "Sheriff West, we really need to stop meeting like this."

Rebecca snorted at that. "Wasn't me this time. That was the fire marshal's call. But if I do need your help, I'll be sure to let you know."

"That's not the whole truth, honestly. I was just yanking your chain a bit. Actually, I was already in Coastal Ridge checking on a few things. When word came of the fire, I raced over as soon as I could." Rhonda stopped, standing close to Rebecca. "And I'm serious, this time. We need to stop meeting like this."

Rhonda's stiff back and heavy tread showed how uncomfortable she was. She and Rebecca had worked together several times already, and they'd done so easily. In the last few weeks, Rebecca thought they'd even started becoming real friends.

Now, looking at her stern face, she wasn't so sure. They'd been on a first name basis up until tonight.

As if to drive the point home, Rhonda stared at Rebecca, her usually cheerful face blank. "Sheriff West, we need to have a talk. And we need to do it someplace private."

6

"How was I supposed to know the fire would spread that fast?" I whispered into the phone. My heart was racing, and it felt like I still couldn't catch my breath. "It was like, things started blowing up, and then the fire just, it just leaped, and suddenly, everything was on fire." Shivering, I hugged myself tightly, trying to calm my racing thoughts.

"Maybe you should've planned things out better." His oily voice dripped with amusement.

This wasn't funny, though. I'd nearly been caught. Everything had gotten totally out of hand as soon as it started.

"I did what you told me to! Just how you told me to do it!"

He laughed at me, and I wanted to puke. The gross smell of gasoline and smoke was all over me. It didn't seem to matter that I'd already pulled off my hoodie. I wished I could have ditched all my clothes, but this man had his own timeline. Still, I'd need to shower soon before anyone noticed the lingering odor.

"I understand you hit that poor sap over the head and knocked him into the hold. Maybe if you're lucky, he was dead before the fire reached him."

Wait. How did he know about that guy?

There was no way I planned to admit to this asshole that I'd left a man to die in the fire. This guy had eyes and ears everywhere. I was never going to be able to escape his grasp if he was this well-connected. And now he had one more thing to hold over my head.

My heart clenched, and my knees went weak.

He hadn't been dead. After he'd fallen down the steps, I'd climbed belowdecks to pull him out. But he was just too heavy. When I'd squatted to grab him, I'd heard his shallow breathing. All I could do was shake him to try to wake him up. But he hadn't even seemed to realize I was there. The fire was going crazy by then, and I was forced to flee.

Once I'd abandoned the inferno and my feet hit the pier, I'd noticed the man's duffel. My thoughts weren't very clear, so all I could think to do was get rid of it. And that was exactly what I did. It was at the bottom of the marshes on the other side of the island.

"I didn't mean to burn that other boat or the dock. These were your instructions. I poured gasoline on the one boat and dumped the oil into the water like you asked me to. So how did it spread to the dock?"

"Like you said, sweetheart, how would I know a fire would spread that fast?" The amusement left his voice, and it was even scarier. If a snake could talk, this was what it would sound like. Cold, heartless, threatening, waiting for me to slip up so it could strike again. "You'd better get a grip on yourself, though, or you're going to end up in jail."

I opened my mouth, trying to think of a way to defend myself. But I couldn't come up with anything. He was right.

I'd screwed up, and now a man was dead. And it was all my fault. This was only supposed to be property damage. Now I had to worry about a possible murder charge.

"Keep your head down. Stick to the plan. You've fucked up enough. Don't go doing anything else. Because the only one who's going to fry for this is you."

The call went dead.

I lowered my phone and stared at the blank screen. He was going to hang me out to dry. I knew it.

Tears streamed down my cheeks as I realized just how screwed I was. Setting fire to the boat was supposed to fix all my financial problems and break his hold on me. Now his grasp around my neck was tighter than ever.

Wiping the tears from my face, I took several deep breaths. He wasn't *actually* choking me. I had to pull myself together. Looking around, I made sure I was still alone, so no one could've heard the conversation.

This was a secret I'd have to take to the grave. And if I didn't play my cards right, that could happen a lot sooner than I wanted. I'd basically made a deal with the devil, and now I had to deal with the consequences.

7

"Coffey and Abner are at the scene waiting for forensics to finish up. Locke isn't on shift for another hour. Melody's at the desk and can't hear us with the door shut. Frost and Darby are off for the day." Rebecca waved her arm around her office, then gestured for Rhonda to have a seat. "This is as private as we're going to get. What did you want to talk about?"

Rhonda sank into the chair across the desk, glancing around. Even seated, she looked stiff, her back straight as she crossed her legs. "I told you I was in Coastal Ridge." She rotated her head, taking in everything she could see in the office.

She wouldn't find much. In the short amount of time Rebecca had been in this position, she hadn't brought in anything personal, and all the former sheriff's belongings had been removed. Other than the books on law and folders of standard operating procedures, there was nothing on the shelves.

"So you said, but you didn't say why." Rebecca sat in her own chair, relaxing back against it.

"I was there for the same reason I'm here now. To investigate Shadow Island's crime rate. Because your town's crime rate has gone up significantly since you came to town."

Rebecca bristled. "Correction. It's the arrest rate that's gone up. You're welcome."

"Sheriff, are you seriously trying to tell me you're not worried about the drastic increase in crimes over the last few months?"

"What's with all the formal 'sheriff' stuff?" Rebecca's heart picked up speed. What was going on here? "Is there something more you're not telling me?"

"Answer my question."

Rebecca noted Rhonda hadn't used her name. "Of course I'm concerned about the crimes happening here. But a spike in arrests is to be expected when laws are enforced after a period of noncompliance. For example, we busted a child trafficking ring...a crime, I'd like to point out, that originated in a different jurisdiction. That took out a lot of people connected with it. We knew that would lead to a power vacuum and all the little shrimps would start coming out, trying to make names for themselves. That also leads to a higher crime rate."

"So it's your defense that this increase is not caused by poor leadership or lackluster performance of your duties but the exact opposite?"

Once again, Rebecca was thrown off-balance by Rhonda's phrasing. "Defense? Do I need to defend myself? We've had crimes. More than usual after kicking the beehive that is the Yacht Club, sure. But my team and I have solved most of these cases. Once we can shake this island free of the influence of organized crime, the rates will drop again, I'm sure of it."

"Then you're the only one. Rebecca." Rhonda leaned

forward, her expression grave. "*Sheriff*. I've been asked to shadow you and figure out why your town is having an unprecedented crime wave."

Ah. Now her discomfort and stilted attitude made sense. Rhonda wasn't there to help or even to visit like they'd discussed doing in the past. She was there in an oversight position on the job.

"Shadow me." It was a statement, not a question. "You'll see we're doing the best we can with the situation we've found ourselves in. I've got one rookie and one that's new to county sheriff work. You know all about that since *you* wrote his recommendation. There's no need for other agencies to watch what we do, but I know you won't find anything untoward within this department. Hell, I've had the FBI come poking their noses in already, and they didn't find anything because we do things the right way."

"Well, I need to double-check the filed reports and provide a more hands-on investigation. I was at the evidence locker, going through the forensic reports involving your town."

Rebecca sat forward in her chair, resting her chin on her clasped hands. "Did you find anything interesting? I've heard stories of cases dropped in the past because evidence went missing."

Clearly, that wasn't what Rhonda had been hinting at, because her mouth snapped shut.

Rebecca shook her head in disbelief. "You didn't know about that?"

"I hadn't heard anything about that."

Rebecca sat back with a grunt. "Damn. Well, check with the courts, then. Several cases were tossed out over the years due to evidence being improperly stored, damaged, or lost."

"You want me to check into your compromised evidence?"

Rebecca shrugged a shoulder, rocking in her chair. "Another set of eyes is always helpful. Why would I mind?" She paused her rocking and leaned forward. Rhonda needed to understand a couple things, so she looked her straight in the eye and made sure the state investigator was focused on her. "I'm a team player, Agent Lettinger. Just don't get in our way."

"I have no intention of holding you back or screwing with how you do things around here. All I've been tasked with is finding out why the reported crime rates have increased dramatically. You hardly go a week anymore without another felony or three being committed."

"*Reported* might be the key word here. My predecessor wasn't much for filing paperwork."

Rebecca thought about all the records former Sheriff Wallace had written but never submitted. He'd filed them away in a cabinet instead, trying to build a RICO case without letting anyone know about it. At least, that was how it looked to her.

It was impossible to be sure since he died before letting anyone in on his plan. He'd been killed by a porter for the Yacht Club when they'd come to pick up an underage teen girl to drive out to one of their "parties."

"What made you decide to check our records?"

"I've been getting a lot of questions I can't really answer. Like, why the state police have had to divert so many resources down here when previously that hadn't been necessary." Throughout their conversation, Rhonda had been easily holding eye contact but now darted a glance at the door.

"Before I got here, they didn't like asking for outside help. And of course, there's the ruckus that happens in tourist towns during peak season. As you know, some of those felons, like the human traffickers and serial killer, came here because of the crowds. Others literally washed up on our shores. Or involved us because you needed our help."

Rhonda sighed, not looking any more at ease than she had been. "Yeah, it was my drug-running case that ended up on your beaches and lost you a good deputy. But the first serial killer was homegrown."

"Spree killer, not serial. And after what happened to his family, even the Virginia Commonwealth's Attorney doesn't want to move forward with charges yet." Deep in her heart, Rebecca didn't blame Robert Leigh for going after the Yacht Club members he blamed for his daughter's murder.

"He's not the only resident who—"

"Yes, we had two residents who lost it and started killing. The third was, again, from out of town. The last one was Coastal Ridge's guy that dropped his body here. The victim didn't even live locally. If you ask me, it's a combination of outside influences."

"You're not worried about this massive increase in crime?"

"I don't appreciate the insinuation." Rebecca didn't see any reason to hide the truth. "I hired more people to handle the workload. We're getting everyone up to speed on how things should work. The tourists are mostly gone, and things will start settling down, or so I've been told. By spring, I'm hoping everyone will be solid in their jobs and things will be much easier."

And, if luck was truly with her, she might even manage to break the back of the Yacht Club. There was no doubt in her mind that the majority of the crimes that happened in town were because of the influence held by that group of rich sociopaths.

Rhonda just pulled her lips back in a grim smile. "Let's hope it works out that way."

8

"Honey, I'm home!"

Rebecca grinned as she kicked off her shoes next to the front door. It felt so good to be able to say that every evening. Ryker had only moved in because he needed someone to watch over him while he was recovering from his traumatic brain injury. Still, it was the first time in a long time she could come home to someone who cared for her.

Ryker popped around the corner, coming out of their bedroom. "And you're barely even late!" Humphrey, an adorable chocolate lab puppy, trailed behind him. He looked up at Rebecca and started wagging his tail, then darted forward and attacked her pant leg.

"Welcome back, Rebecca. Was the paperwork from the fire just dreadful? Not something you needed on a day like today." Meg Darby, Deputy Viviane Darby's mother, walked out from the kitchen. Viviane, her daughter, was the first person who'd reached out to make sure Rebecca felt like a part of the community, but Meg was second. Like mother, like daughter.

With Rebecca's hectic work life, it was impossible for her

to spend all day with Ryker. Yet someone had to be around him in case his short-term memory loss returned, as it had on several occasions. To solve that issue, she'd asked the few friends she had on the island, and they all took turns coming over to sit with him while she was at work.

When Ryker had been settled into Sand Dollar Shores, Rebecca had gently questioned him about why his parents weren't tending to his recovery. They'd been overprotective in keeping her from him while he was hospitalized, yet now they were noticeably absent. His detached response had simply been that they were traveling.

"Thursdays are always weird days with the new training schedule." Rebecca cuddled up to the puppy, then leaned into the hug Ryker gave her. Humphrey whined at having his access denied by the embrace. She looked down at him and got a nip on the chin for her troubles. But he licked her face, and she forgave his puppy bite as she scooped the growing dog into her arms.

Ryker's forehead wrinkled in confusion as he ruffled Humphrey's ears, trying to distract him from his daily attack on Rebecca. "Um, what fire?"

Rebecca sighed, watching Ryker with concern. "Babe, I told you about the fire down at the docks. Remember? We were sitting together on the deck and noticed the smoke..." She paused to give him a chance to remember. Anxiety rippled through Rebecca, and her fingers tightened in the warm fur of her canine companion.

"That's right. You..." Ryker narrowed his eyes as he tried to focus. His body tensed, as if he was trying to force the memory to come to him. His breath came out in a rush, and he shook his head. "I got nothing. Nothing. I don't remember that conversation at all."

Ryker slumped in defeat, and her heart went out to him.

He'd been struggling with memory loss for more than a month now after cracking his head. Most days, he was perfectly fine. Other days, he would forget a random thing. There was never any telling when it would strike, which was the reason he was staying with Rebecca despite the newness of their relationship. They'd only been a couple for a few weeks.

"Did you remember to take your pills today?"

Meg opened her mouth to answer but pinched her lips shut as Ryker brightened.

"I did. That I remembered. I ate a tomato sandwich for lunch, and then I took my pills." He stared at the older woman. "Right?"

"Right." Meg beamed at him. "You did say you were tired earlier. That probably has something to do with you forgetting."

He rubbed his temple. "I was really tired."

"Is that why you were in the bedroom? Are you feeling better now?" Rebecca inspected his eyes as they crinkled up in amusement.

"I was taking a nap but feel fine now. I think," his eyebrows jumped up, "yes, we did discuss the fire at the docks. You got a call and had to rush off. Then I guess I sat here worrying. When Meg came by and updated me, I was so relieved I nearly passed out. That's when I went to bed."

"Your discharge paperwork did mention that you could have lapses in memory when you're stressed or tired. And you were both," Rebecca reassured him. Humphrey wiggled to be let down. As big as he was getting, it was hard to hold onto him when he got the notion to be free. She released him, and he scampered off to sniff something.

Out of the corner of her eye, she saw Ryker frowning. His forgetfulness was a minor nuisance to her or Meg, but it had to be gut-wrenching for him. Not being able to rely on your own mind must've been terrifying.

Rebecca *tsk*ed. "I'm sorry you were worried."

Ryker rolled his neck from side to side. "No, don't apologize. Life is going to happen. It's better that it happens here where you guys can help me than at home alone when I won't notice. Don't even think about it." He grinned, hugging Rebecca into his side. "I'd like to hear your version of what happened at the docks."

"Why don't we talk while we eat?" Meg gestured to the kitchen. "Our sheriff hasn't had dinner yet. Have you, dear?"

"No, ma'am." Rebecca held up her hands, covered in dog fur and saliva from where the pup had chewed on her.

"Then go wash up, and I'll get the table set." Meg shooed her off and turned to Ryker. "You make yourself comfortable at the table while I dish up Pastor Brett's Mexican casserole."

"You're going to stay and eat with us, right, Meg?" Rebecca headed for the bathroom to wash her hands and face. By the time she was finished drying off and had put on a clean shirt, the food had already been served, and she slid into a chair at the dining table.

Humphrey was happily hopping with his back legs as he gobbled down his bowl of kibble.

Rebecca and Meg took turns explaining what had happened. For the most part, Ryker nodded along, not asking many questions. He spoke up when Rebecca described the yacht that had been anchored near the docks, however.

"That sounds like Oswald Chapman's boat. What was his boat doing down at Dee's place?" He lifted his glass of water and took a drink. Due to his condition, he'd stopped drinking alcohol, even just a single beer.

In solidarity, Rebecca was also drinking only water with

her meal. "No clue. We weren't able to get in touch with him yet. We called and left messages with all the boat owners. So far, none have responded."

"Well, it was late in the day." Meg pointed with her fork at the clock on the wall. "Not everyone takes phone calls after dinnertime. We used to not do that. In fact, I remember a time when it was a social norm not to bother people at home between five and seven. And it was downright unheard of to do so after nine." She shot a mock angry glare at the cell phone Rebecca had set on the edge of the table.

"It's only for work, ma'am. If I wasn't the sheriff, I wouldn't have it out at all. Or I'd be playing music with it. But with all the things that have been happening, I'd rather be safe than sorry."

"There've been an awful lot of odd occurrences recently." Ryker pushed the rest of his food around his plate. He'd barely eaten half of what he'd been served.

He wasn't eating as much as he used to. The man had an active job and ate enough to keep up with it. Maybe it was only because he wasn't currently working while he recuperated. Rebecca hoped that was the reason, at least.

"Lots of stupid people try their luck when they think the new guy won't be able to fill the shoes of the last man." Meg nodded sagely, looking back and forth between them to make sure they were listening. "Thankfully, we've got ourselves a wonderful, smart, justice-driven sheriff to put those idiots in jail as soon as they start causing problems."

And look where that got me...a babysitter from the state police.

Feeling her cheeks heat up, Rebecca shook her head. "I'm not sure if that's the reason, or if it's because I irritated the Yacht Club. Either way, someone thought it was a good use of state funds to send a special agent from the General

Investigation Section of the Bureau of Criminal Investigations down here to make sure I'm doing my job properly."

"That's not a good look with the elections approaching." Ryker grabbed her hand under the table. "Do you think that's going to hurt your chances of keeping the job?"

"Oh, *psh*." Meg waved her hand. "Nobody who matters and is paying attention will see a statie here as anything other than a good thing. Hell, I might even spread the rumor that Norfolk sent that woman down here to get training from our fine sheriff."

They laughed at that. Humphrey, done with his meal, crawled under the table and curled up on Rebecca's toes. Meg knew everyone worth knowing on the island. And as a member of the Select Board, she had a lot of influence as well. But it was not as much as Richmond Vale, the chair. And he hated Rebecca for standing in his way too many times when he thought profit mattered more than justice.

For a moment, she wondered if he could be the reason for the oversight from the state. But she quickly brushed that thought away without speaking it. One, she didn't want Ryker to worry. Two, she was beginning to think Vale didn't have that much clout. And, three, considering his suspicious activities, she doubted he'd intentionally draw additional scrutiny to the island.

If it hadn't been Vale who pulled strings to get Rhonda to look into her case, then might it have been someone else in the Yacht Club? Since they hadn't been able to take her out with illegal methods, perhaps they were trying the legal route now.

Anything was possible with that group. And it would make it much harder for Rebecca to fight them.

9

Rebecca trailed behind her deputies as they made their way through the station door. She smiled as Viviane continued ribbing Hoyt.

"I can't believe you asked for a bag of doughnuts to go, Frost. How greedy can you get?" Viviane waved to Elliot as she approached his desk.

Today was a day of remembrance for the 9/11 attacks, and Bean Tree Coffeehouse was giving out free doughnuts and coffee to emergency and medical workers. It was an annual event they hosted to honor those who risked their lives in the aftermath.

Rebecca had been touched by the banners with all the names of the firefighters, doctors, nurses, and even boat captains who had put everything else aside to go to New York and help with the cleanup and searches. She hadn't been surprised to see Wallace, Hoyt, and Greg named on banners, nor the Darbys.

Walking into the station, she felt a sense of pride in the men and women she worked with. "He deserves those doughnuts, Darby. Let it go. Besides, they were free, and you could've gotten some to go as well."

"I'm not saying he doesn't deserve them, Boss. I'm just wondering where he plans on putting them." Viviane rubbed her hands over her belly. "I'm so stuffed I might just go take one of the cruisers out and have myself a nap in the sun."

Elliot Ping grinned from the dispatch counter as they walked in. His gaze tracked the bag Hoyt was carrying, even though he wasn't so blatant as to lick his lips. With the number of people who'd shown up for the memorial that morning, every doughnut had been hot and fresh when it was served. The two dozen Hoyt had brought back with them smelled like heaven.

"You sound jealous, Vi. Not my fault you didn't think to ask for some yourself." Hoyt swung the tantalizing sweets in front of her nose.

Viviane pouted and pushed the bag gently away as Rebecca unlocked the half door that kept civilians from just walking into the back offices. "It's because I don't have any more room. But how am I going to sit here and smell those and not eat them? I'll be distracted all morning."

Hoyt laughed and slid the bag across the counter to Elliot, who jumped guiltily. "Grab yourself a couple, kid. I didn't forget about you being stuck here and unable to partake with the rest of us. Unlike some gluttons."

Viviane stuck her tongue out at the back of Hoyt's head where he couldn't see her.

Rebecca fought to choke back laughter as she held the door open for the rest of them to walk through. The younger woman had practically grown up at the station. Viviane's mother, Meg Darby, worked as dispatch before Viviane stepped in. Now Viviane was a deputy and would probably never leave the station until she retired. Hoyt had been like an uncle to her for years.

Though Vi had grown up and joined the force, the dynamic of their relationship was unchanged. They were constantly picking on each other. Jake Coffey, the newest addition to their troop, watched the interaction without saying a word, but amusement danced in his eyes—pale-blue like a husky's.

The front door opened again, and Rebecca turned in time to see Rhonda Lettinger walk through. One hand carried a box of grocery store doughnuts balanced atop a folder while she tried to juggle two drink trays in the other.

"Well, hey, Agent Lettinger. I didn't realize you were planning on working here while you're overseeing us." Rebecca gestured, and Jake turned around to help take the top tray of coffee cups.

"I come bearing gifts, so don't be too angry with me." Rhonda started to lift her offering, then saw the cruller on the counter and Elliot with powdered sugar on his lips. "Um, but it looks like you've already eaten."

Hoyt picked up the bag of doughnuts he'd brought in. "And these are so much better than those. Try one."

"Well, I brought some good coffee, at least." When Rhonda stepped forward, Rebecca hit her key fob, unlocking the door to admit the special agent. She didn't want Elliot to get sugar all over his desk.

"Guys, Special Agent Lettinger has been asked to come down and review our cases. Someone seems to think we've had a bit too much crime recently."

"You mean other than all of us?" Viviane smirked, then took the second tray of coffees from Rhonda. "Always good to see you again, Lettinger. Let me help you take these into the bullpen."

"I have to admit, I didn't expect such a warm reception, considering why I'm here." Rhonda peeked into the Bean Tree bag. Her eyes widened as the steamy sweet perfume hit her nose.

"Grab a doughnut and come join us. I was just about to get everyone caught up on our latest case." Rebecca saw she was nearly drooling with anticipation.

"Is the dock fire going to be a case then?" Hoyt folded himself into his chair.

Viviane set her load on the table next to the coffeepot. "It's not just a fire. Someone died as well."

"And as far as I know, it hasn't been ruled either an accident, suicide, or murder yet. This is a general death investigation. Bailey should be tackling the autopsy soon." Rebecca spied how quickly Rhonda finished off her first doughnut and moved on to her second, which looked to be one of the new triple chocolate ones.

"Do we know if there were any more bodies found?" Jake settled in his chair and turned on his computer. "They hauled off the boats, but we didn't hear back before I left for the night. The divers were still working, but they were with the staties on the boat."

"No more bodies. Just the one found on the *Shoreline Catch*, a charter fishing boat owned by Cole Fairbank." Rhonda licked the chocolate glaze from her fingers as she steered the conversation. Opening her folder, she withdrew a picture and used a magnet to post it on the whiteboard. Clearly, Rhonda had been reviewing the case while they'd been at the remembrance ceremony and breakfast.

"And the body wasn't Cole?" Viviane asked.

Rebecca held up her hand to stop that line of questioning. "Until we hear from Bailey or Cole himself, we won't know that. Last night, we called the owners of all three boats. None of them answered. Considering Elliot didn't hand me any messages—"

"I swear I don't have any." Elliot had stepped in to grab a doughnut.

Rebecca waved him and his pastry back to his desk. "Then they haven't called back yet either. The other two boats that burned were the *Look Around* and the *Liquid Asset*. That last one is owned by Oswald Chapman. We have no ID on the body or even a guess. It was primarily skeletal remains semi-coated in melted boat parts."

As Rebecca said the names, Rhonda pulled out photos and added them to the board. She also attached a picture of the corpse that had been found in the *Shoreline Catch*. After working with a skeleton crew for so long, the bullpen felt crowded with five people in it.

Rebecca had thought Rhonda agreed not to interfere. Having her actively working with them was off-putting and honestly a little annoying, considering why the woman was actually there.

"Special Agent, do you plan to stay here for the entire case?"

Rhonda took another bite of her doughnut, frowning around it. "I didn't *plan* any of this, Sheriff West. But my bosses want answers. And let's face it, your crew has been running thin for a while now."

"Was. We're fully staffed now." Rebecca's rebuttal was immediate. She didn't like the idea of anyone criticizing her people, not even Rhonda.

"And that's still not enough to reach the suggested staffing guidelines for a town this size that plays host to so many tourists. But two of your people are new, and one's fresh out of retirement. And don't think I don't know that another one of your deputies is being retrained because he screwed up for years." Rhonda used a thumb to gather a flake of icing and pop it into her mouth. "Everyone knows about him."

That was something Rebecca had feared. Once Deputy Trent Locke had turned his back on the Yacht Club members who pretended to be his friends, they'd started a nasty smear campaign against him. The worst part was, it was built on truth. It had already taken a toll on Locke's self-esteem.

Hoyt interrupted them before they could really argue, reading aloud from his computer monitor. "According to the fire marshal's preliminary report, 'the fire was likely started between four thirty and five yesterday evening.'"

Viviane looked thoughtful. "Seems odd to try and get away with something like that at that time of day."

Hoyt continued reading, enunciating like a newscaster for his assembled audience. "'While there were certainly people in the area at the time of the fire, not many noticed anything wrong until the smoke got their attention. By the time people did notice, the first ship and part of the dock were already burning. With tourist season over and hurricane season ongoing, the boats aren't as active.'"

Jake looked up from his desktop. "No one we spoke to yesterday was even sure if the fire started on the pier and then moved to the boat or the other way around."

Rebecca finished writing the names of the owners under each picture. Realizing she was gripping the dry-erase marker too tight, she took a calming breath before turning around. Rhonda was paying attention to everything they were doing. With someone scrutinizing their every move, it was nearly as bad as being back in the FBI.

"But the third boat wasn't tied to the dock or attached in any way. So how did it catch on fire?" Rhonda's voice made

Rebecca's muscles tense involuntarily. "Could it have been from a fuel spill of some kind? I did see puddles of fire on the water they had to put out."

Rebecca took a step away from the whiteboard, barely glancing at Rhonda. "We'll need to hear back from the marshal or forensics to find that out. Until then, I want the three of you to find the owners. Make sure they're alive, first and foremost, since none of them are returning our calls. After that, see if they can think of anyone who would want to burn their boats. Or if they've had any problems with kids playing with fire recently. That was another thing the witnesses at the dock didn't know anything about."

"Speaking of, Boss, we didn't find the one who pulled a runner yesterday." Hoyt kept his gaze on Rebecca, as if showing Rhonda he trusted her. "But the staties found a purple hoodie tucked into the dumpster of a consignment shop two streets down from where you lost them. It's been sent in to forensics. They're going to look for anything they can get DNA from to try and identify who it was. I put it all in my report that I turned in this morning night."

"Good. I don't know why they ran, so I'd like to track them down and ask them some questions. Also, I viewed my personal pen video footage, and it wasn't any help with identifying them or offering clues to where they went. And I didn't see any other out of the ordinary activity."

"Uh, Boss." Elliot was desperately trying to flag Rebecca down from his chair. "Richmond Vale is here to see you."

10

Knowing how this would go, Rebecca turned on her pen camera. "Lettinger, would you care to join me?" She tapped the list she'd made on the board. "The rest of you, boat or person, I want to know if there was any reason to destroy them."

Rhonda followed as she walked to the lobby.

If Richmond Vale was here in person, it could only spell trouble. Though she had to admit that face-to-face or over the phone, he was just as much of a nuisance. The man could put hemorrhoids to shame with the way he was always crawling up her ass.

He was standing at the half door, leaning against it while sputtering at Elliot to open it.

"Only employees, witnesses, and criminals past that point, Mr. Vale. Since you're none of them, we can speak right here." Rebecca stopped three feet short and stood tall with her hands resting on her hips. "Is there something I can do for you?"

"You can figure out who burned my friend's boat! That's your damn job! Why aren't you doing it?" Vale's face was blotchy, and froth formed along the corners of his lips. After working himself up yelling at Elliot, he was now loosing his anger on his favorite target.

Rebecca moved to the side slightly so Rhonda could have a front-row view of his antics. "Is Cole Fairbank your friend? Or are you talking about Perry Ballard?" She suspected neither of them had ever even had a friendly conversation with the head of the Select Board, but it was fun to poke at his pride.

He started shaking his head immediately, his short, styled hair not even swaying with the amount of product he'd used. "Who? No, I'm talking about my good friend Oswald Chapman. His favorite small yacht was one of the ones that burned. Why aren't you down there figuring out who did this to him?"

"Because I'm in here, having to talk to you instead of figuring out who burned three boats and killed a man. We're following up on—"

"I don't want you following up on anything!" Spittle flew from his lips. "I want you to do your job and arrest the person responsible for burning Oswald's boat. He's very upset by this."

Rebecca was glad she'd kept her distance as she watched another spray of saliva fall to the floor.

"Mr. V—"

"If you were any good at your job, this wouldn't have happened in the first place." He glared at her, looking proud of his jab.

"Are you implying this case is linked to another case I was already working on?" Rebecca fought to keep from smiling at his slip.

"What? No. What are you talking about?" Vale spluttered, pulling back.

She shrugged, feeling let down that he hadn't incriminated himself or anyone else. "Unless this is related to another crime, I couldn't have stopped it before it happened. As an officer of the law, I'm only allowed to arrest people after they've committed crimes. Not before."

"If you hadn't brought this crime wave with you when you became sheriff, then people wouldn't think they could get away with even more crimes. That's where you've failed us. And that's why this happened." Vale, unable to physically reach her, shook his finger at her instead.

Funny that he shows up screaming about the crime wave I'm supposedly responsible for while Rhonda stands here investigating me for that very thing. Maybe I've underestimated him.

"Do you have information proving that this was anything more than an accident?" Rhonda stepped forward, mirroring Rebecca's posture.

A trace of a smile briefly danced across Vale's face. He leaned forward and gestured at the shorter woman.

"Finally! With the crime rate so bad, I'm glad to see a higher authority was called in to deal with things." He looked down his nose at Rebecca. "Perhaps you could sit this one out and let the *professional* handle the case. Since you showed up, our crime rate has skyrocketed. As the head of the Select Board here on Shadow Island, I have to say I'm very disturbed by this growing trend. I wouldn't be in the least bit surprised to find out this was no accident."

Well...that answers that question. Maybe Vale had enough pull with the staties after all.

Vale turned back to the special agent. "I believe with this case in your competent hands, you'll find out who destroyed a very expensive vessel owned by one of the most prominent families in our town."

"Mr. Vale, we're in the middle of a murder investigation.

Are you suggesting we instead focus on why your friend's boat suffered some damage?" Rhonda's tone was much softer than the one Rebecca would have used.

His smile was back, and he was all charm with Rhonda. "I'm sure you're more than capable of doing both. She hired extra deputies. She's fully staffed. And now that you're here, perhaps we can all get some answers. Find out who the killer is, and you can also determine who set fire to the *Liquid Asset*. With you heading up the investigation, I'm confident we'll get answers."

Rebecca didn't understand the apparent lovefest Rhonda and Vale were sharing, but she couldn't spare too much consideration for the matter. She had a more pressing issue. "Tell me something, Mr. Vale. How did you even learn about Oswald's boat? Because we've been trying to call him since last night, but he hasn't picked up once or returned any of our messages."

"Only his friends call him Oswald." Vale looked down his nose at her, having to tilt his head back to do so. "And he told me about it himself on the phone."

"And did he happen to tell you why his very expensive yacht was anchored near a dock filled with working boats? Or how it happened to get there only hours before a fire was started?"

"I believe he mentioned he needed some repairs done and that the marina repair shop is especially busy at the moment." He waved off her question, glancing away, as if it, and she, were beneath him. "I don't know how or when it got there. Oswald's a very important and busy man. I'm sure he had one of his employees take it down there for him."

"Hmm, would you make an official statement saying as much?"

Vale's mouth snapped shut, and he shook his head,

pulling himself up straight in a vain attempt to look taller. "That seems a little...unorthodox, doesn't it?"

"Taking witness testimony after the fact? Not at all. I'll even take you back into the office so you can make a full statement." Rebecca hit the buzzer on Elliot's desk, unlocking the door and pulling it open for him. Elliot did his best to look absorbed in paperwork, but she noticed his shoulders jerk as he coughed to hide a laugh.

The head of the Select Board stepped back, straightening his tie. "I'm a very busy man. I don't have time for such nonsense. If you were a competent sheriff, you'd have known all this already."

"That's fine." Rebecca swung the door shut with a bang. "I planned on going out and having a talk with *Oswald* soon. Should I tell him you send your regards in this trying time? What about the family of the deceased? Anything you'd like to pass on?"

"Why would you need to see Oswald in person?" Vale's wild antics stopped, and his forehead developed deep furrows as he frowned.

To his credit, Dick really does seem confused.

"Because he sent you down here to make a fuss about his yacht. Guilty dogs bark the loudest, you know." Rebecca maintained eye contact while they spoke.

"If you're looking for guilty parties, then you should talk to Serenity McCreedy." He sneered as Rebecca failed to keep the surprise from showing on her face. "She's got a real thing against influential people. Bring her in and ask her to give a statement."

Knowing her pen camera was still running, she hoped she could nudge him over the edge. "Why do you believe a seventeen-year-old victim of assault is a credible suspect in this case? And why do you think she has a grudge against 'influential people?' The man who attacked her and killed her best friend was a businessman who owned a modest company. Is there something you know about her case from this past summer that you never came forward with, Mr. Vale?"

"Just do it!" Vale spun on his heel and stormed out the front door, shoving it open with more force than necessary.

Both women watched him through the tinted glass as he stomped up the street and out of sight.

"Why would he think that Serenity would have a grudge against Oswald Chapman?" Rhonda leaned to the side, getting closer to Rebecca and keeping her voice low.

Rebecca snorted. "'Grudge' isn't the right word. Serenity tried to blackmail a Yacht Club member named Owen Miller when she learned he murdered her best friend, Cassie Leigh. Last I knew, she skipped town."

"Sounds like that may have changed."

"Indeed, it does." Rebecca turned to head back to work. "Which means I need to find her before the Yacht Club does."

11

"I'm not cleaning up that mess." Viviane waved her hand to the front where Vale's voice could easily be heard. "That nasty little troll spits all over the place when he yells. Mama says they have to wash the tables off after every Select Board meeting."

"Don't worry about it. It sounds like Rebecca is wiping the floor with him already." Hoyt sat stiffly in his chair and kept glancing down at his shirt pocket.

Viviane narrowed her eyes, trying to see what he was doing. She knew him well enough that his body language was unnaturally rigid. If he were a woman, with his shoulders pulled back even though he was seated, she'd think he was trying to adjust his bra or get a free drink at a bar. Then it dawned on her. "Are you recording them?"

Hoyt looked at her out of the corner of his eye, careful not to turn his chest where the pen camera was tucked into his pocket. "You bet I am. After what he's said and done in the past, I want to make sure all our interactions with him are recorded."

"What are you two talking about?" Jake had turned in his chair, frowning inquisitively.

It suddenly occurred to Viviane that she wasn't certain if Jake knew about the spy cameras they carried in place of body cameras. Worse, she wasn't sure if he *should* know about them. She shot a look at Hoyt, hoping he knew how to handle the situation.

"Vale thinks he's the top authority on the island and can't stand the reality that he's not. Since Rebecca took over, she's not let him run roughshod on us the way he used to."

"The way he still wants to," Viviane clarified.

"He does some really questionable things, but he also has access to our spending. Boss got spy cameras on the down-low that look like pens." Hoyt pointed at the pen in his breast pocket, careful to keep his hand away from the lens. "If she hasn't gotten you one yet, I bet it's on order."

That cleared that up. Hoyt trusted Jake. Viviane wasn't ready to go that far yet. She didn't distrust him, per se, but her jury was still out. This circumspection was a holdover from her years of working the dispatch desk. She heard a lot and talked about little of it.

In contrast, Hoyt had always been a bit too open like that, no matter how many times he regretted it later. She decided to change the topic. "How are we going to go about interviewing the three people whose boats burned? Boss asked us to focus on them."

"The fire marshal hasn't stated which one was the original source of the fire. Sheriff asked us to start with the one not owned by Chapman." Jake smoothly transitioned back to the case.

He didn't seem all that worried about the underhanded way they were forced to act because of the corrupt politician. Maybe he was used to it. Or maybe he thought it wasn't a big deal. He hadn't seemed especially worried about the Yacht Club either.

When she'd learned the legends were true, Viviane had nearly broken down. Then again, she'd grown up immersed in the stories instead of hearing them only as an adult. "I can go talk to Cole Fairbank about the *Shoreline Catch*. He and his wife have a place in town and are probably awake by now and should have gotten our messages. Frost can go—"

"Senior Deputy Frost," Hoyt tapped his chest, "your training officer, can go with you because you're still a rookie. This isn't like when I let you go talk to Deborah on your own. Get used to it. You'll be doing interviews with me for the foreseeable future unless I know for a fact the person you're talking to isn't a suspect in the case."

Viviane crossed her arms. "And how did you know Deborah wasn't a suspect? You didn't know she was out of town until I came back and told you."

Frost raised one eyebrow at her, and she knew she'd put her foot wrong somehow. "Because I follow her on social media, and she was at a convention getting her pictures taken at the time of the murder. If you were as experienced as I am, you would've checked that before heading over to talk to her in person."

Viviane immediately deflated. The classes she'd passed to become a deputy hadn't been hard, and she'd scored high in every one of them. Her background helped a lot with her tests. Now that she was working the position, though, she was catching on that there was a lot said and done by the others she'd never paid attention to. And that was all stuff she had to start doing on her own now. Being reminded of that was a bit humbling.

"Yes, sir. You're right." She took a deep breath and grinned at Hoyt. "Good thing I've got you looking out for me. How about you and I go talk to both Fairbanks and Perry Ballard instead." Jake was staring at her, and she narrowed her eyes. "You got a problem with my idea?"

"No, ma'am. I've just never heard you call anyone 'sir' before, and it threw me off. I'm still trying to get to know you all." He pursed his lips. "I have to say, I'm glad to hear you're not one of those hotheaded rookies who goes running off after every lead because they're certain they won't ever be in danger."

Viviane's cheeks heated. Out of the corner of her eye, she saw Hoyt's lips twitch as he fought against a smile. She had done precisely that once already. But the butt-chewing she'd gotten from Rebecca and Hoyt had been enough to convince her to never do it again.

Thankfully, they both believed in "reprimand in private, praise in public." If she didn't mention it to Jake, it was likely no one else would either. Later, she might know him well enough to share that. Right now, she just wanted to get on with the job and not think about it.

Rebecca and Rhonda walked back in, and she relaxed, shifting attention to them. "Hey, Boss, Frost and I are thinking of heading out to talk to two of the boat owners since they haven't returned our calls yet. Did you and Jake want to tackle Oswald Chapman? That could become a political nightmare I bet you'd love." She grinned.

Rebecca stopped in front of the rows of desks to look at them all. "No. Vale was sent here to yell about Chapman's yacht, and he tried to gloss over the death and the other two boats involved. Vale's interest is...worth noting. But let's stick with multiple investigative prongs."

Rhonda's head tipped to the side as if she wanted to say something but was smart enough to keep her mouth shut. The other woman was there because some paper pusher thought Rebecca wasn't doing a good enough job, and Viviane did not care for that one bit.

The sheriff continued as if there wasn't an investigator staring over her shoulder. "Jake, follow up with the fire marshal and see if he's got anything for us. Darby, you and Frost take the two commercial boat owners. Keep your radios on and let me know if you see Vale or anyone else harassing them or even hanging around. The Aqua Mafia always messes things up, so let's try to keep this one as clean as possible."

Jake inclined his head. "Yes, ma'am."

Rebecca took in a deep breath. "With that said, let's not get tunnel vision. Though this case stinks of the Yacht Club, there are other possibilities too. We need to explore each and every one of them. Got it?"

Viviane stood and grabbed her hat, ready to go. "Got it, Boss." Once she got in the cruiser, she could send her mother a message. Maybe together, they could find out who'd sent Rhonda down here and why.

Rebecca might've considered Rhonda an ally or even a friend in the past, but Viviane wasn't so willing to trust the special agent. Not when it came to her dear friend Rebecca. No one was going to make her boss look bad while Viviane Darby was around.

12

"Looks like you were right." Hoyt gestured at the open windows at the residence of Cole and Addison Fairbank. The owners of the *Shoreline Catch* were some of the victims of the fire they needed to speak with. "Someone is home, at least. I wonder if they've listened to their messages yet."

Viviane stepped out of the SUV, finally putting her phone in her pocket. She'd been tapping away at that thing so hard, he'd started to worry she'd end up with bruised fingertips. Her hands drifted around her belt, touching every pouch. "He's in. So why didn't he call us?"

He looked at her, searching for further signs of nervousness. She'd sounded so cocky and sure of herself at the station. Had he been too hard on her, calling her out for wanting to interview alone?

It was such a hard line to walk with training rookies. They had to be confident enough to act, but not so sure of situations that they put themselves in danger. It was a lot like raising kids. He'd done a decent job of that...mostly thanks to Angie.

But he'd never had to send either of his sons into a kill-or-be-killed situation with guns drawn.

Swallowing hard, he waved her toward a path of decorative pavers leading up to the front door. The path was surrounded by a stamped layer of concrete, textured and painted to look like sand with seashells mortared in place. And in the middle of their small front lawn was an election sign supporting Rebecca and Meg Darby.

At least they have a lick of sense.

Viviane waited for him to join her before knocking on the door.

Mrs. Fairbank, an attractive young woman with unusually smooth and unblemished skin, answered the door. "Hello...oh, Viviane. It's you. Did you need something?"

Stepping up into the shade of the covered porch, Hoyt realized the woman's youthful appearance was a ruse aided by a thick slathering of makeup. For a moment, he'd forgotten she was in her mid-thirties. Makeup sure had come a long way over the years.

Angie would've scolded him for classifying a woman in her mid-thirties as not young, but Hoyt viewed everyone through the lens of his sons' ages. If someone looked younger than his boys, they were youthful. If they were older than his boys, they weren't. He knew it didn't make sense, but he didn't care.

Mrs. Fairbank blinked, fluttering unnaturally long eyelashes at him as a rainbow of colors shimmered from her eyelids.

He guessed people would consider her makeup artfully applied, but it was obvious she'd covered every inch of her face. Maybe raising two boys kept him from understanding why women found all of it so necessary.

"Good morning, Mrs. Fairbank. Is your husband here?"

Addison brought her hand to her throat. "Is this about Cole's mom?" Her voice dropped to an unsteady whisper as she spun around to check behind her. "Has something happened? Come on in."

Hoyt held up his hand, stopping Viviane from stepping inside. Her reaction seemed a little too well rehearsed. "Happened to his mother? No, not that I know of. We're here about his boat. Did he get our phone calls?"

He moved up beside Viviane, using his height to look over Addison's shoulder. The house was picture perfect, if a bit spartan. A simple couch sat along one wall with a coffee table in front. A flat-screen television had been mounted on the opposite wall. In the middle of the room stood a tripod with a circular lamp mounted on it.

"His...boat? Oh, thank goodness. His mom's health has been failing recently and when I saw you..." She waved that off as the smile returned to her face. "Cole's having some coffee in his office. You can come in. I could get you some coffee too." She stepped back and gestured for them to follow. "Cole, baby, the police are here to talk to you about your boat."

Viviane waited for Hoyt to give the nod to follow. Addison left a line of dots in the thick carpet, her pointed high heels digging deeply into the pile. The background research they'd done of her social media accounts didn't indicate any job other than helping out with her husband's business. She was too overdressed for that.

And heck, Cole was working from home anyway. Maybe her attire had something to do with that weird circular light fixture. Lots of people were working from home these days, and he couldn't keep up with all the new technology.

They followed her, stopping in the front room as

Addison entered the dining room and called for her husband again. "Cole, can you come here, please? It's really important." She turned to face them, clasping her hands at her waist. "I don't want to startle him the way you guys startled me."

"Babe, what is it?" A dark-haired man wearing a ragged button-up shirt and cargo pants stepped out of a door just off the dining room. "I was on the phone with the insurance company. I can't help you with whatever shot you're trying to do now." He stepped around the dining table and stopped abruptly when he saw Hoyt and Viviane. "Right. You here about my boat?"

"Mr. and Mrs. Fairbank, yes, we'd like to talk about your boat." Hoyt introduced himself and Viviane.

Cole sank into a chair, dragging a hand through his thinning hair and pushing it back from his forehead. "Please. Have a seat. I got your message about it this morning."

Addison pulled out two chairs from the table, then stepped into the adjoining kitchen. "I'll get that coffee."

Hoyt leaned over the chair to see what she was doing as Addison busied herself near the coffeepot. He didn't want to overdo it, but he knew Viviane would watch his every action so she could model proper procedures.

"Then you understand that we have a few questions for you." Viviane took one of the offered chairs and turned it so the kitchen wouldn't be at her back.

Hoyt was pleased to see Viviane automatically assessing her environment so well. Law enforcement officers always avoided turning their backs on suspects and witnesses, no matter how innocent they seemed. He did the same, pushing his chair back so he could keep both Cole and Addison in view.

When he glanced around the house, Hoyt found a surprising pile of household junk tucked behind the couch. There was even a disassembled recliner hidden away there, with the back resting flat on the seat. Everything was tucked out of sight behind the couch, but the mess was only hidden from one direction.

"Your boat, the *Shoreline Catch*. Have you always docked it at Dee's?" Viviane pulled out a notepad.

Hoyt casually reached for his shirt pocket to make sure the button on his pen was down and still recording.

"Since I bought it seven years ago." Cole ran a thoughtful fingertip along the table's wood grain. "Had my last one docked there too. Dee always treated me right, and the customers don't get distracted or dawdle walking through his place. We can just get on the boat and go."

"And if they forgot any supplies before leaving, they can buy them from Cole while they're out." Addison picked up a wicker tray with a lighthouse-themed coffee set arranged on it and brought it to the table. Before taking her seat, she stepped back and snapped several pictures with her phone. She was so thorough about getting all the angles, Hoyt wondered if she was auditioning for a part on their forensic team.

To her credit, Viviane kept an eye on the woman's every move. "When was the last time you took your boat out?"

Cole didn't seem to notice his wife's interesting behavior, or maybe he was used to it. "Took it out two days ago. Wednesday evening. Night-fishing trip. We came back early Thursday afternoon. One thirty, I think it was."

Addison finished her photo shoot and took a seat, leaving the steaming cups on the tray, just out of everyone's reach.

Viviane shot Hoyt a confused look. "Mrs. Fairbank, I hope you won't think I'm prying." She used her megawatt smile. "Could you tell me why you're taking so many pictures?"

Addison started to speak but snapped her mouth shut when Cole answered instead. "She's trying to start an online marketing business. Has a real knack for it. She does tend to go a bit overboard, though. Did you see all the stuff piled behind the couch?" He glanced into the other room, shaking his head.

Hoyt put the pieces together. Though he didn't understand how taking pictures of things translated into a marketing business, he was glad Viviane had asked about the woman's behavior. "I did notice. Reminded me of my boys when I'd ask them to clean their room and they thought I wouldn't check the other side of their bed." He chuckled to let them know he meant no disrespect.

"Exactly!" Cole slapped his hand on the table, rattling the coffee tray.

"Well, that sounds very exciting." Viviane's smile still radiated as she spoke with the woman.

"Thanks. It is." Addison adjusted her artfully messy bun. "And I'm sorry about the junk. I have to project just the right image during my videos, and I can't have a bunch of clutter in the background."

"But babe, it makes the house so sterile and unwelcoming."

Addison clenched her jaw, the vein in her temple pulsing even as she smiled at Cole. Hoyt hoped Vi's question hadn't started an argument that would derail their inquiry.

As if reading his thoughts, Viviane moved the conversation back to the boat and the night of the fire. "Well, good luck. So we don't keep you any longer than necessary, I need to ask, did you see anyone hanging around the docks at that time?"

Viviane tensed as Cole half stood in his chair to pass out the tiny cups of coffee, leaving the saucers on the tray. "Not anyone unusual. Dee was there, of course. I said hi to him. Um, I think Ty was there, the mechanic. I heard him tinkering in the shop and asked him to gas up my boat for me." Cole pulled a sugar packet and a single-serve, nondairy creamer cup from the tray before retaking his seat.

Worried the thin handle of the teacup would break in his fingers, Hoyt gingerly set his cup down.

Across the table, Cole stirred the sugar and cream into his coffee while Addison began recording the act, swaying her phone back and forth with the movements.

Hoyt wanted to snatch her phone away and tell her to pay attention.

Instead, he cleared his throat. "Was your boat low on gas or did it have no gas when you left it?" Hoyt rested his forearms on the table and clasped his hands together, getting their attention. Sitting like this, the pen in his pocket could not only record audio perfectly, but it could also capture Cole's expression.

"Nearly empty." Cole stuffed the empty sugar packet into the creamer cup, creating a tidy pile of trash. "She holds more than eight hundred gallons of fuel. You can see why I didn't want to wait around for her to get refueled. I had to go see my mom, and Ty's never shortchanged or overcharged me. So I always tip him well."

"Who were your customers?" Hoyt looked over to make sure Viviane was still taking notes.

"A group of guys from Tennessee. Frat brothers a long

time ago just wanting to reconnect and hang out on a boat for a couple of days. I can get you their names. They disembarked about two hours before me. I had to clean up and get things put away, so she'd be ready for the next booking."

"You got any more customers lined up?"

Cole sighed. "I do. But now I don't know what to do with them. I have a second boat that's smaller and older. It has the necessary gear I'd need, but I'm not sure it can handle a group their size. I suspect I'll have to cancel their reservation. The damage to the *Shoreline Catch* is bad, and I'm not sure yet if it can be fixed."

Hoyt dug a little deeper. "Is that why you were on the phone with your insurance company before you called us?"

"Yeah. Got to protect my livelihood, ya know? Those two boats are all I have. And with the primary boat down, my business is going to take a serious hit."

"What kind of insurance policy do you have on it?" Hoyt watched Cole's face intently.

Cole looked up from his coffee. "Nearly a quarter-million. That's how much it would take to replace her."

"Over a third." Addison didn't bother to look up from her phone as she corrected him. "We raised it a few months ago, remember?"

Viviane flipped a page in her notepad. "Why did you raise it?"

Cole hooked his thumb over at his wife. "Babe, you want to explain to the police why we raised the insurance payout?"

She finally set her camera down. "It was because of the hurricane and all the weird crimes happening. Plus, Cole's been doing really well this year, and we can afford it. Lowered the deductible too. Like he said, we can't afford to have anything happen to that boat. The other boat is much smaller and can't really handle the size of groups we book."

"And the policy is three hundred thousand now?" Viviane asked.

"Three hundred twenty-five thousand is how much it would cost to cover the rest of the loan, get a new boat, pay our bills while we're down a boat, and get the new ship fully kitted out...and the tank filled." Addison ticked each item off on her fingers. "We might be able to offset some of the lost income with the smaller boat, but it isn't as cost-effective."

Considering her preoccupation with her phone since they'd arrived, Hoyt was surprised she was even listening, let alone so knowledgeable about Cole's business. From everything he'd seen about Shoreline Excursions and the *Shoreline Catch*, the whole operation was under Cole's name and control. A few of her social media posts had mentioned helping Cole, but those had seemed more like one-offs rather than regular contributions to the business.

Cole smiled at his wife with pride. "My wife is a numbers woman. She keeps the books straight and everything running smooth. All I have to do is run the boat. My Addy keeps everything neat and organized so I can do the labor-intensive work. I couldn't run my business without her." He kissed her knuckles without glancing over at her.

Hoyt watched the couple carefully. *On the surface, they seem to have a good relationship. But underneath?* He suspected this wasn't real love, respectful love. He was certain, without having to see it himself, that Cole would smile at his boats with the same amount of affection. *This was the love a man had for a possession, not a person.*

For her part, Addison blushed. It was like she blossomed under the light of his attention. "It's no big deal. I just pay the bills when they come in and make sure the reservation money is higher than the expenses. Anyone could do it. I manage it all from home while I handle our bills. He's the one who runs the company."

Viviane grinned at the couple. "You know, I've heard the Vikings considered math a form of magic, and one that only women could do properly. That was why women ran the households and the businesses."

Addison's eyes widened, and she snatched up her phone. "I love that. Mind if I write it down?"

"Go ahead." Viviane nodded at the device before turning her attention to Cole. "Tell me about your work, your boat."

"Fishing's fishing." Cole shrugged. "The cabin's nice enough to have guests. I can sleep in the galley, no problem. If we get someone wanting to pay to go out with me and the money's right, I'll take them. They don't mind if I do some fishing too. Double pay if you have a good run, selling the fish to the market and getting the tour money too. Plus, Addy figured out that if I fish, I can show them how it's done right. Half the time, they end up buying some of my bait off me and giving me a decent tip for offering advice."

Addison glanced up from her phone. "He's a very good fisherman."

Cole turned to Viviane. "The insurance agent said I need a case number in order to file a claim. Do you happen to have that information? I was going to call you to ask about it before you arrived."

Viviane nodded and pulled a card out of her back pocket to write on. "Cole, where did you go after you left the dock?"

"To visit my mom. She's in a hospice facility by the hospital in Coastal Ridge. Mom has advanced liver cancer. The cancer's going to kill her, but with the treatments, she can live a little longer, at least." He took the card from

Viviane and tapped it on the table. "If we can keep paying for them."

As Hoyt watched Addison squeeze her husband's hand, he felt sorry for the couple. First a dying mother, then a dying business. Maybe the woman's photography was her way of maintaining control in her spiraling world.

13

Sitting in her cruiser, Rebecca rolled her head away from the view of the McMansion where Oswald Chapman lived. It was very telling that it was located only a few houses down from Albert Gilroy.

Depraved birds of a feather flocked together. As far as she was concerned, everyone in the Yacht Club was morally perverted. Even if the person wasn't actively committing crimes, turning a blind eye made them guilty by association.

Rebecca spoke into her phone. "Tell Chapman we have his yacht in our evidence garage. If he wants to know why or what happened to it, we'll be by later to talk to him. If he's not available then, I'll try to schedule him in sometime later this week."

"He's not home, I take it?" Rhonda asked from the passenger seat of Rebecca's cruiser.

"According to his assistant, *Mr. Chapman* won't be available until after noon today."

Rhonda pulled down her seat belt and secured it. "Do we want to go back to the station, or do you have something else to do while we're out?"

Rebecca turned the key in the ignition, thinking through all the other possible leads. "I had a witness who took off at the docks before I could question them. They disappeared in the business area just to the north of there before I could get a good look. Some troopers found their purple hoodie tossed in a garbage can behind one of the stores. I'd like to talk to the store owner."

"Why the owner?"

Putting the transmission in drive, Rebecca drove around the loop that made up the Chapman driveway. "Because a lot of people around here have security cameras. The hoodie was how I tracked the suspect through the streets. If it was in the dumpster behind the store, then they must have taken it off."

She couldn't quite keep the edge of irritation out of her tone.

Rhonda's fingers drummed on her armrest. "You don't have to get angry with me just because I'm doing my job."

"I'm not." Rebecca glanced over at her passenger. Rhonda's jaw was tight but not clenched. She also wasn't looking at Rebecca. "I'm getting annoyed at the stupid questions we both already know the answers to. Why would I talk to the owner of the store where we found evidence? Really, Rhonda?"

"Hey, I'm not the bad guy here."

"Neither am I. I'm also not a trainee, a newbie, or a rookie. Nor am I stupid. So please, don't condescend to me. I've worked cases across the country. And I'm damn good at my job. My record speaks for itself. In the FBI and with the quagmire I've found myself in here."

Rhonda twisted in her seat to look at Rebecca. "That's true. So tell me, why do you think there are so many more crimes now?"

Did she really need to spell it out again?

"Like I said before, I think it's a two-part problem. The crimes, for the most part, were already here. They just weren't being reported. I moved the rock the cockroaches were hiding under, and now they're all scrambling." She sneered, unable to help herself. "Honestly, if the staties and VCA had done their jobs properly, most of these problems would've been taken care of years ago."

"You're saying this is our fault?"

"I'm saying I have records for an awful lot of arrests that were thrown out of court because of improper handling of the cases once they left our island. And that problem went on for years. Eventually, Wallace stopped even bothering because he knew whose cases would never be tried." At a stop sign, Rebecca turned to face Rhonda. "Did you check into those? Did you look into the outrageous incompetence happening in those evidence rooms?"

Rhonda opened her mouth but didn't say anything.

"Maybe you should go back and find out. Ask whoever sent you down here why no one investigated when all those cases were tossed out of court. Why no one investigated when the reported crime rate dropped nearly overnight."

"What do you mean when it dropped? When did that happen?"

"Look it up." Rebecca slid into the on-street parking not far from where she'd met the state troopers the night before. "This isn't me giving you a hard time or trying to prove anything. I just want you to be completely unbiased by my theory when you see the evidence I saw."

Rhonda reached for the door handle. "You want to give me a time frame to look at?"

Rebecca sipped her coffee while she thought about it. "Look at the years there was a change in the sheriff's office."

She paused and had another idea. "And when the Select Board got new members."

"I'll do that. And I'll check into the missing evidence and dismissed cases too." Rhonda started to open her door, but Rebecca grabbed her arm.

"I have a list of names that'll get you started." She let go of Rhonda's arm and climbed out of the SUV. Rhonda followed suit.

The special agent took her time walking around the parked vehicle, and when she did, she moved to stand in front of Rebecca, blocking her path across the street. "If I find what you're suggesting, then we'll work together to sort out the bullshit. I'll hound my supervisors. I'll interrogate anyone who pushes back." She had to lift her chin a bit to hold Rebecca's gaze, but it was rock steady.

Rebecca had felt so sure of herself in the cruiser, so vindicated in turning this inquiry back on the ones who'd called for it. But the reality of the situation hit her like a brick. "You might not want to do that, Rhonda. I did the same thing in the FBI. Look where that got me. And these guys aren't playing around...just ask Alden Wallace. They're willing to kill to sexually exploit teenagers and to traffic illegal substances. And they have a literal fleet."

"And I've got Crips trying to move into my neighborhood and a serial killer who's sworn to find me and gut me like a fish." Rhonda rolled her eyes as if she didn't have a care in the world. "Not to mention I eat gas station sushi." She checked for traffic, then headed across the street.

That last one made Rebecca grimace and clutch her stomach. "I knew you were a badass, but damn, girl. Even I won't touch gas station sushi anymore." Rebecca followed after, trying not to remember the horrible state she'd woken up in after that ill-conceived food choice.

Rhonda laughed, and the tension that had been building between them all morning evaporated. "Anymore? But you *have* done it." She opened the door for them to Second Place consignment shop.

"Well, yeah. Sometimes that's all that's available during a late-night stakeout." Rebecca looked around the shop. There were tall racks running from the front of the store to the back. Each was chock-full with an assortment of small, mundane appliances and toys mixed with any type of clothing or book you could ever want.

"Do it a few more times, and you'll build up a tolerance. I'm sure you'll learn to love it." Rhonda's eyes sparkled with mischief as she assured her, reminding Rebecca of Viviane.

"Did I hear someone is loving something?" A woman wearing a patchwork vest and bohemian-style skirt stepped out from between two of the aisles.

"She's loving gas station sushi. And I am not." Rebecca pointed to Rhonda, who dipped her head in acknowledgment, before pulling out her badge. "I'm Sheriff Rebecca West, and my food poisoning-loving friend here is Special Agent Rhonda Lettinger from the State Police. Mind if we ask you a few questions, Ms...?"

"I'm Chantel Reed, the owner. And I'm with you on the food poisoning, especially since fresh seafood is right there in the ocean." She pointed over her shoulder. "I've got a sushi-making kit, complete with instructions, if you'd like to take a look."

Rhonda brightened, but Rebecca spoke before she could. "Unfortunately, we're here on official business. We found a piece of evidence in the dumpster behind your shop. Is there any chance you have cameras that might have caught who went back there last night?"

"Of course." Chantel turned and wiggled her fingers,

indicating they should follow her. "People were using our dumpster all the time when they brought in stuff we just couldn't sell. Like, no one wants threadbare or ratty clothes, you know. No matter how many times I warned people, they'd still go around back and toss their garbage in my bins. I finally had to get a motion-activated light and security camera installed back there."

Rebecca reached the counter and realized that Rhonda was lagging behind. "Did that work, or do I need to have my guys patrol this area more often?"

Chantel smiled. "Oh, you're so sweet. But no, the spotlight is enough to get them to scatter, even during the day. Now I usually just use the camera to watch them freak out and try to run away. It's better than YouTube some evenings."

Rebecca grinned. "I bet."

Behind the counter, Chantel tapped on a tablet screen. "You said last night? Doesn't look like we had many. Only five videos. The camera is motion-activated too. Oh, here you go, this should be the one you're looking for." She lifted the tablet off its dock and turned it around for Rebecca to see as Rhonda wandered up to join them.

On the video, a hooded figure had just come into view, already pulling the hoodie off.

Rebecca tilted the screen to remove the glare from the overhead lights. "This is the person I chased." She was surprised at how clear the image was.

The hooded figure walked into the alley, then startled when the motion-activated light switched on before eyeing the area. After looking all around twice, she finished yanking the hoodie off, exposing shoulder-length blond hair. Manicured nails raked the hair back into place as the woman lifted the lid to the bin and ditched the hoodie. She then turned around, facing the camera, and leaned around the corner of the building.

"Do you know that girl, Sheriff?" Rhonda had to stretch her neck to see over the raised counter.

Rebecca did, and the face she was looking at shocked her. It was Serenity McCreedy. Vale had been right. Shadow Island's prodigal daughter had returned.

"Anything else I can help you ladies with?"

As Rebecca began to ask for a copy of the video, Rhonda set something on the counter.

She then pulled out her wallet. "I'll take the sushi-making kit."

14

For at least half an hour, I huddled next to one of the massive piers still standing after the fire I'd set, shifting from foot to foot, constantly looking over my shoulder. I knew acting like that only made me look more suspicious, but I couldn't help myself. It was the middle of the day, and I was literally hiding in shadows waiting to talk to him.

How had I gotten myself wrapped up in something this...stupid? I should go home, tell him what I'd done, and ask him to help me find a way to fix it all. He said he loved me. Sometimes, I believed him. A few times, I even tried relying on him. But then he'd leave again, and I'd be all alone. Left with everything my body needed to survive, but nothing more. I felt like the family pet being left at the kennel while the rest of them went on vacation.

And I was expected to stay, be a good girl, and then get all excited when he came home again. Until he went on his next work trip. Because there was always another business trip. He would take time off for the other women in his life, but never me.

I'd wanted a change, and now I was standing in the shadows waiting on a different man to finally decide whether he had enough time for me. At least I could watch the water. It was so much like me. Ebbing and flowing around the pillars of the pier, moving around all the obstacles humankind put in its way.

Damn, I had to shake it off. Just forget the fact that I'd killed a man and move on. I clenched my jaw to suppress the sobs that tried to overwhelm me.

Just keep smiling.

Because that was what I did. That was what a good girl did. I smiled and found a way to put on a brave face.

Except the cops were everywhere. Ever since the lady sheriff arrived on the island, the people who committed crimes weren't getting away with them like they used to. The smile began to slip from my face.

"Hey there now, don't lose that pretty little smile of yours. You must know by now that things will be fine in the end." Wet sand shifted underfoot as he finally joined me.

"Things are not *fine*." My words hissed through my gritted teeth. "They will never be fine again."

"Why not?" His grin would've been right at home on a snake.

Seeing that, I knew I never should've trusted him. Never should've taken him up on his offer. My mom would be so disappointed in me if she were still around. "Because we killed a man."

"You." The smile dropped from his face, and his eyes went as cold as a reptile's. "*You* killed that man. You burned his body. This is all on you. Don't try to pin your actions on me. All I did was offer you the opportunity for a better life, which you asked me for."

I clenched my fists at my sides. "I didn't think it would

turn out like this." Anger bubbled up, and I welcomed it. Rage was a needed break from beating myself up over something I couldn't change.

He shrugged so casually. "Neither did I. But that's what happens when you send a girl to do a man's job."

My arm jerked with the urge to slap that smug, condescending smile off his face. "I did the job. We're even now."

"Not so fast." He had the nerve to reach out, as if he were going to grab my arm. I pulled back, glaring at him. "Bad news for you. The fires didn't totally take out the yacht. That means you still owe me."

I stared at him, shocked to my core. "I...I don't have any money to pay you back!"

His eyes slithered over me, and that serpentine grin returned. "I never said it had to be money. It can be other things. There's more than one way to make a buck."

My skin crawled at his suggestion, and my body twisted in disgust as I drew away from him. I might have screwed some creeps in my day, but there was no way I'd do anything with this sleazeball.

"Not interested? Then either give me the money you owe me, or I'll send you out on another gig. It might be delivering packages. Could be holding something for me until I need it again." His eyes once again drifted over me—this time, devoid of lust. "Considering your tendencies toward violence, I might just send you the next time I need somebody offed."

Bile raced up my throat, and I had to cough to keep it down. *Yeah, there are things he could make me do that are way worse than sleeping with him.*

"Don't forget, I know what you did. I know why you did it. And I know exactly who to tell if you ever think of trying to get away. You go back and live your life, but remember, until you pay me back in full, I own you."

He turned and walked away like I was nothing.

I wasn't worthless. I was *not* something to be owned. Anger filled me, stronger than I'd ever felt before. I wanted to chase after him and claw his eyes out. But he just kept walking.

If there was more than one way to make a buck, there was more than one way to cancel a debt.

In for a penny, in for a pound.

15

"As if I needed my day to get any worse!"

Hoyt had gotten harsher greetings before when walking into an office, but never from someone who wasn't his boss. Or his wife. Or from Darian. Okay, maybe a lot of people greeted him like that. He wouldn't take it personally, though.

"And good afternoon to you, too, Perry."

"Afternoon, Mr. Ballard." Viviane stepped through the door of the Shadow Boat Tours office behind him, waving cheerily to the grumpy man as he slammed papers around on a desk.

The office was swaddled in glossy pictures of tanned, smiling people on boats, waving up to the camera or pointing at breaching humpback whales. The decor and vibe clashed horribly with the puckered, scowling face of the owner and captain of the *Look Around*.

It also was in stark contrast to his black hair, gelled back so thickly that it reminded Hoyt of a Ken doll. And of Vale, now that he thought about it.

"I've already lost my boat, my livelihood, and will most

likely lose my house too because of it. Are you here to interrogate me until I confess to burning down my boat?"

"That depends." Hoyt crossed the small office to the desk. He was surprised to find that Ballard maintained his office on this side of the island. This was a high-rent district, the beaches taken up by mansions worth millions. While this street wasn't exactly on the sand, it was still damn close. To him, it seemed silly to try and offer your boating services to people who probably owned a fleet of yachts already.

"On what?" Ballard narrowed his mud-brown eyes.

Hoyt pulled out one of the cushy chairs at Ballard's desk and sat down. "On whether you set your boat on fire."

"Why the hell would I do that?" The man popped out of his seat but dropped down just as quickly once Viviane stepped closer.

"Insurance scam? Got too drunk? Lost your temper and did something stupid?" Hoyt listed the reasons he could think of right off the bat. Given Ballard's behavior, he was betting on the last one.

"Insurance? Ha!" Ballard sent papers skittering across the desk, though not so hard they fell onto Hoyt's lap. Maybe he was capable of controlling his temper after all. "I've been trying to locate all the receipts I need to file my claim. And you know what I've found out?"

"Nope." Hoyt rested his chin in his hand, elbow propped on the arm of the chair. His quiet nonchalance was working well enough to get the guy talking.

"That my insurance won't cover my boat's repairs! It sure as hell won't cover replacing the damn thing! Do you know what that means?"

This time, Ballard did fling some of the papers onto Hoyt's lap.

"Go ahead, read it. That's my deductible. That's what I

have to pay. And that doesn't even touch all the upgrades I put into it. My bar. The extra head. Sightseeing equipment." He shook his fists at the pile of papers in front of him.

Hoyt started assembling the paperwork that had landed on his thighs, browsing through the documents as he went. Ballard certainly was hot-tempered and didn't seem to think things through very well. Those could be qualities of an arsonist and murderer.

Or just a dumbass.

"Why did I settle for the cheapest insurance available?" Ballard stormed on. "My deductible is massive. If I had that kind of money, I wouldn't need the damn insurance. Thought I was being smart by keeping my premium low. But apparently, I'm a moron, thinking something like this could never happen to me. I'm ruined."

Viviane squatted down to pick up the pages on the floor. "I think what you're telling me is that you'd have no good motive to burn your boat."

Ballard squeezed his hands into fists, pressing them against his temples. "Of course not! I had a contract coming up. A very wealthy family. They wanted a two-day tour. Not an overnight, but two back-to-back days. Influential too. I would've gotten so much publicity." The angry rant trailed off to a whine. "I'm going to have to return all the deposits I took too."

Hoyt finished reading and stacked the papers together into a neat bundle. "If you didn't do this, do you know of anyone who would want to ruin you? Or destroy your boat?"

"If I did, you'd be dealing with a lot more than just a fire. You'd also have a murder on your hands!"

Interesting. Does he know about the charred body we found?

"A fuse that short, and you don't have anyone who wants

to get back at you?" Viviane's question was so innocently stated but packed a punch.

Ballard collapsed face-first onto his desk. "No one. Everyone knows I rant and rave, but never with a customer. I have a five-star Yelp rating. I've never hurt anyone that I know of either. Not since I was a kid at least, and that friend, his name is Stan, never held it against me. In fact, we're still good friends to this day. So the only person I ever wronged sure doesn't seem to be too bent out of shape about it."

Viviane twisted to shoot Hoyt a stare.

He shrugged. Ballard's overly dramatic face was still buried in his paperwork. "One more question, Mr. Ballard. Can you tell us where you were between five and seven yesterday evening?"

"Sure can. I was helping that same friend move. Stan had already gotten most of the boxes packed but needed help with his furniture and his damn oak bed frame that only breaks down into three pieces." He lifted his head from his desk. "And the matching bedside tables."

"Do you have a last name and phone number for Stan the owner of the damn oak bedroom set?" Viviane pulled out her notepad.

Instead of answering, Ballard reached for his desk drawer. Before Hoyt could do more than tense up, he'd yanked it open, reached inside, and slapped a business card on the desk in front of Viviane. "There ya go. If you don't know where you're going or how to get there, just ask Stan. He'll get you where you need to go."

Hoyt's muscles relaxed, and he let out a breath he didn't realize he'd been holding. Having a suspect you're questioning suddenly reach for something out of your sight line was just one of the reasons Viviane wasn't allowed to interview on her own. He glanced up at her and saw that she still had her palm on the butt of her gun, the holster snap undone.

She saw him looking and smoothly slid her hand to her back, acting as if she were scratching an itch. Ballard hadn't even noticed.

"He owns a taxi company? Your friend, Stan." Hoyt flipped the card over and read the back. *If you don't know where you're going or how to get there, just ask Stan. He'll get you where you need to go.*

"Did. He's retired now. Last week, in fact. But the number's the same. He'll vouch for me. Hopefully he'll help me move, too, when I lose my house." Ballard dropped his face back on his desk with a hollow *thump*.

"Well, take this. You'll need it for your insurance." Viviane set her card with the case number on the table.

Hoyt stood and headed for the door. Viviane was right on his heels and blew a sigh of relief when they stood in the warm sunshine again.

"I nearly drew down on him."

He nodded, glancing over at her. "You did. And that's a good thing. We had no way of knowing if he had a gun in the drawer or anything else. Best to be safe. And I was seated, couldn't get to my gun fast enough. Thanks for having my back in there." Hoyt patted her on the shoulder, and she beamed up at him.

Suddenly, she was the tiny little girl with puffy pigtails again, excited to get his approval.

"Does that mean I get a strawberry shake?"

Back when Meg Darby had been their dispatcher, and he'd just been an uncle figure who could spoil a little girl, her mother had warned him that using food as a reward would come back and bite him in the ass one day. He grinned. "Damn straight. That's the rule, right?"

"Right." Viviane turned for the cruiser, nearly skipping with excitement. But that sentiment fizzled away fast when she came to an abrupt halt, her attention focused on something in the distance.

Hoyt turned to find what she was staring at, then groaned. "What the hell is she doing?"

Addison Fairbank stood not fifty feet away, holding a gadget out in front of herself. She was smiling, adjusting her hair, looking over her shoulder, sidestepping this way and that. Rinse, repeat. She looked positively looney.

"She's not foaming at the mouth yet, but my dad always warned me about critters that act like that."

Viviane elbowed him in the side. "Hoyt Frost," she pursed her lips in a failed effort to hide a big smile, "are you suggesting that woman has rabies?"

"It would explain a lot." He grabbed her elbow and pushed her forward so she could lead the way. "You go ask her. Just make sure not to get any saliva on you. That's how it spreads."

She dug in her heels. "First, you know she's starting an online business. What she's doing over there isn't all that different than her behavior at her home. Second, what happened to not interviewing witnesses solo?"

"You're not going alone, but you *are* going first." He nudged her forward as he fell in step directly behind her, watching Addison's behavior closely. Of course, if he'd thought the Fairbank woman was a credible threat, he'd never make Viviane take the lead, but the woman's "influencer" behavior was akin to dealing with some of the everyday crazies they encountered.

"Addison, hello. What are you up to?"

Addison startled, nearly dropping her selfie stick, and huffed in annoyance. Her eyes scanned around until they landed on Viviane and Hoyt. He hung back a few steps, pretending to be on his phone.

If things go south, I can always tase her.

"Well, hey there, Viviane. I didn't see you. I'm just using this selfie stick to get a good video with the boats behind me. My followers will want to know about this recent tragedy and how they can help." She made a sad face. "They love knowing what's going on in my life, and this is just too big not to share."

"Your followers?" Hoyt looked around as he pocketed his phone, but of the few people out and about, none of them were paying any attention to her.

Viviane rolled her eyes at him. "Stop being so clueless. She's just recording a video."

"Right." Addison smiled sweetly. "For my social media pages."

Hoyt wasn't a fan of social media and didn't understand the allure of posting every single aspect of a person's life for others to either swoon over or criticize. In his opinion, nothing good resulted from broadcasting one's every move, as it only invited unwanted scrutiny and eroded the value of personal privacy.

Or maybe I'm just an old fart who doesn't get it.

He'd had his own privacy invaded and shared around himself. Photography of the honeypot set to tarnish his reputation almost ruined his marriage, after all. Why anyone would want to do that to themselves on purpose was beyond him.

Hoyt glanced at the phone at the end of the stick, wondering if the video was still rolling. From what he could tell, it wasn't. The screen showed a still image of Addison's face with the Seaview Marina directly behind her. It was a good distance away, but at the right angle, she could line up her camera so that her background was littered with expensive yachts.

He scratched his temple. "If this is to talk about your husband's boat burning, then why aren't you filming at Dee's, where it happened?"

Addison rolled her eyes skyward, her head shaking almost imperceptibly. "Well, because if you want people to take you seriously professionally, you have to appear to be successful. Nothing says success more than a fleet of yachts as your backdrop." She waved her hand behind her, indicating the view.

Hoyt was still trying to connect how pictures of coffee would help her make money. He then decided to switch topics to something he understood well...questioning suspects and witnesses. "I forgot to ask, Mrs. Fairbank, did you go with your husband when he was visiting his mother?"

Addison looked shocked at the question. "With him? Oh, no, I was working. Mama Fairbank has gotten self-conscious since the chemo. She's not much for visitors, except for Cole."

"You work with your husband, then? I thought you said you only balanced the books for him." Viviane tilted her head.

"Cole hardly needs me to work for his company, so I'm starting my own. Like I told you before, I work from home. Online marketing and social media management." She beamed with pride.

"I thought you said the boat was the only income you two had." Viviane waved her pen between Addison and her phone.

"I did. And that's true. My business is brand new. I'm not making any money yet, but I'm confident big things are going to happen soon. I'm just finishing up some content before we make our grand reveal and start signing clients." She smiled at the camera and took another picture. "Right now, I'm letting people get to know me so I can build my platforms before I begin rolling out products."

"We?"

"Oh, I have an assistant." She lowered her stick, plucking her phone from the holder. "Speaking of whom, I need to get back to work. She's waiting for me so we can get today's videos edited and uploaded."

As they watched her scurry off, Viviane leaned close to Hoyt. "Frost, I know people try to make money this way, but you can tell me the truth. Did you set it up so the people we interviewed were part of a super-sneaky way to haze me?"

Hoyt laughed. "Nope, these are just your usual, run-of-the-mill oddballs." His grin fell away. "And we have to figure out if one of them killed a man."

16

Rebecca pulled her cruiser into a parking space. It was after one, and she and Rhonda were in front of Oswald Chapman's office. In contrast to his posh residence, this location gave off strip mall vibes, sandwiched as it was between a smoke shop and a vacant store with a *For Lease* sign in the window. Considering that Chapman was basically a loan shark, Rebecca found the location fitting.

She'd just shut the engine off when her phone rang. "West speaking."

"And this is Bailey speaking." The medical examiner was as chipper as ever. "You have time to talk?"

"For you, Bailey, always." Rebecca gestured at the phone, and Rhonda nodded, mouthing the word, *Speaker*. Rebecca pushed the button and laid the phone on the console between them.

"I should just add you to my speed dial, considering how often I call you. That would make things much easier when I need to update you on one of your victims."

Rebecca flinched as Rhonda speared her with a look. "You're on with me and Special Agent Lettinger from BCI."

"That makes things easier, then. I won't have to call Rhonda and repeat myself. She's already on my speed dial." Bailey laughed. "How're you doing, Rhonda? Did that new Thai place turn out to be any good?"

Redeemed, Rebecca interrupted before Rhonda could go on one of her foodie tangents. "We're sitting in the car about to go grill a suspect. Do you think you can give us the condensed version of your report?"

"This is only the preliminary report, so sure. Your victim was a male, six-five, mid-forties, with brown hair. His head had been submerged in a puddle of water, so that part stayed intact when I got him."

Rebecca swallowed hard. If his head was intact, the implication for the rest of his body was not good.

"Thankfully, I can say he died of smoke inhalation and not from the flames. Though the fire itself did a number on him. It's hard to burn a body, since we're mostly water, after all. But it was hot enough to burn through all skin layers, exposing bone in the thin spots."

"Thin spots?" Rebecca didn't want to ask the question.

"His wrists and ankles, for example. He had a contusion on the back of his head."

The back of his intact *head.*

"Considering where it was and the position he was found in, I think he was hit by something, rather than landing on something. He could have easily been rendered unconscious by that blow. If luck was with him, he was passed out until he died."

"Anything we can use to identify him?" Rebecca opened her onboard laptop and started entering the victim's description into the file.

"Not yet. I've sent samples off for DNA testing. Find me

something to compare it to, and I can answer yes or no only."

"Bailey," Rhonda scooted closer to the phone, "did you find any signs of a struggle? Did the victim fight back at all?"

There was a long pause on the phone, and Rebecca furrowed her eyebrows and stared at Rhonda. Apparently, Rhonda wasn't getting the full picture.

"Uh, Rhonda, most of his body except for parts of his head and back were burned down through the muscle tissue. If he hadn't been protected by the stove door, I doubt we'd have anything left of him at all. I have nothing to look at to tell you whether he defended himself or not."

"Can you send along photos? I don't know why I haven't gotten them yet."

Rebecca bristled at Rhonda's passive-aggressiveness.

"I can do that." Bailey's voice hinted that she was aggravated too. "Though I can't tell you why you don't have what you don't have."

"The reason you don't have the photos is because I wasn't the one taking the pictures this time." Rebecca kept her attention on the laptop as she spoke. "For safety reasons, the fire marshal ordered that the boats in question be towed in, then only he and his techs had access inside. They took pictures, and I had to get mine from his office. They're in our case folder now, if you'd like to take a look. There aren't as many as usual, but they're sufficient. I also took video of the scene, which is uploaded."

"Rebecca's my go-to for any pictures of the scene if I need to make sense of the bodies." Bailey's addition was enough to tip the scales, and Rhonda sighed and put her phone away.

"It sounds like I need to get caught up. Thanks for letting me know, Bailey."

"Anytime. You ladies have fun today, and if you decide to go out for beers tonight, I'm available."

Rebecca made a noncommittal sound and thanked the M.E. before ending the call. She switched on her pen camera. "You ready to meet Chapman now?"

If Rhonda noticed, she didn't react. Instead, she nodded and opened her door. "Let's get this done, so I can call my office and find out why I'm not getting timely updates." She slammed the door behind her.

As mad as she might've been at being caught flat-footed, Rhonda still waited for Rebecca to join her before walking in.

They entered through the glass front door to find a sparsely furnished reception area. Two molded plastic beige chairs had their backs to the plate glass window. Between them was a short table with *Architectural Digest* and *Bon Appétit* magazines carefully fanned with their titles on display. It struck Rebecca as humorous that Chapman felt those titles gave legitimacy to his profession, though she doubted any of his clients did more than glance at the glossy photos.

A man with jet-black hair and a wrinkled blue shirt bobbed his head as the two women entered. They didn't even have to show their badges as he rose to his feet behind the desk with a faux wood top. He didn't speak as he led them to the only other door, which he courteously held open.

"Ah, the infamous lady sheriff. I hear you're the reason my beautiful yacht was destroyed in a fire." Oswald Chapman leaned back in his pleather chair and eyed her up and down. His curly light-brown hair matched his perfectly trimmed goatee. The square glasses he wore made his eyes look small and beady.

Rebecca had been prepared to shake his hand. Now she was glad she hadn't tried. From the way his eyes crawled over her, she worried she'd have to count her fingers if he got his hand on them.

"I assure you, I have a solid alibi for the time of the fire and when we suspect it started. I am not the reason your boat burned. What about you, Mr. Chapman? Do you have an alibi? Where were you between five and eight p.m. yesterday?"

"He didn't tell you? It's shocking how little you know about the important happenings in your town, Sheriff." Chapman waved off her question as if it mattered not at all. "I was with my good friend Richmond Vale on his yacht the *Golden Apple*. We were discussing our mutual opposition to a new zoning ordinance that would dampen potential growth in the town."

"By potential growth, do you mean profit in your pocket?" He hadn't offered them a seat yet, and Rebecca was more than happy to remain standing. Blood, guts, and even bile didn't bother her much any longer. But she knew if she sat in one of his worn upholstered chairs with wooden armrests, she would end up feeling dirty.

"My good sheriff, all growth generates a profit for those of us who are prepared to take risks and invest in it."

"Not everyone benefits from the kind of growth you're talking about. Some people end up negatively impacted and find themselves in financial hardship. You know the kind of growth. A developer decides he wants some property, and palms get greased. Next thing you know, the hardworking people who live there are being bought out for pennies on the dollar of what their property is worth or threatened with eminent domain."

"Now, you listen to—"

"Have you done that recently?" Rebecca rested her fists on his barren desktop, leaning forward. "Used sudden changes to zoning laws to force people into making decisions that put them in your debt? Developed any new enemies or dragged up old ones from your past?"

He stroked a finger over his mustache while twisting back and forth in his chair. "Every businessman has enemies. It's part of the job. However, I do not have any whose names stand out. Those who try to act against me tend to not be a threat for very long, if ever."

Rebecca straightened. "That sounds a little menacing. You don't think some of the people you've loaned money to at astronomical interest rates might have had reason to try to strike back?"

"No." Even his snort of derision sounded chunky and foul. "None of them would do something as asinine as setting my boat on fire when I wasn't even on it. What would it gain them to destroy one of my toys?"

"You weren't on it, and it was parked at Dee's Dock instead of in your usual, prepaid slip at the Seaview Marina. Why is that?"

"I planned to take the *Liquid Asset* out for a long cruise. To get away from colder weather and storms for a while. Before taking it on a long excursion, I always ensure that it's been fully checked to make sure there are no issues. It's a terrible thing to become stranded on the ocean. No one can hear you call for help."

As threats went, his was cleverly worded and classy. Rebecca wondered how long he'd worked on it, or if he just had a lot of practice. "The Seaview has a full staff of trained mechanics with experience working on boats of your size and caliber. Why not use one of them?"

"Because I'm not the only one who had the idea to get

away for a while. Several of the others did, as well, and the wait times for a mechanic were simply too long to bear. I decided it would make more sense to take it to a different mechanic. That way, I could help a small business. Community growth, like I mentioned earlier. I've heard that Ty down there does excellent work."

"So you're saying it was just a coincidence that your yacht happened to be there in the short window of time when a fire broke out. And was also, coincidentally, close enough to the two burning boats to ignite."

He shrugged, causing the padded shoulders of his suit jacket to almost cover his ears. "Terrible luck, but life is strange, Sheriff. So is the ocean. You can never predict what's going to happen next."

Rebecca wondered if his oily smile actually worked on people. "Which is the reason people get insurance. Mr. Chapman? Did you have insurance coverage on your yacht?"

"I do." He stroked his chin, smoothing the whiskers of his beard. "Not enough to cover replacing it, but enough to pay off the loan on it. Not a good business decision on my part, I admit. But it wasn't my main yacht either."

"Then you're saying you'll end up losing money?" Rhonda butted in, and Rebecca's eye twitched at the intrusion.

"I will. A goodly amount of it. I'll be taking a significant loss on this tragedy. I had several pricy things onboard as well. Those, I assume, are also destroyed." He held up one finger, as if to stop them from speaking, even though neither of them had started. "And before you ask, my insurance doesn't cover the replacement of any personal items on the vessel either."

"Why were you taking your secondary boat on your extended trip? Is something wrong with the other one?"

He swatted the air as if Rebecca were a mosquito buzzing around his head. "No, no. That one is more for large gatherings, parties and such. It isn't suited for long voyages."

Although she was recording the whole interaction, Rebecca jotted pertinent comments on her notepad. "Do you think someone might've tried to destroy it to hurt you financially? Or maybe just a way to smear your reputation. A possible rival gang?" Rebecca glanced at Rhonda, careful to keep the pen aimed at Chapman. "Is it still called street cred if they do all their deals on the water?"

"Rival gang?"

She turned back to face Chapman's shocked sneer.

"Yeah, you know, some other gang that would want to take out the competition. After we busted that child smuggling ring, it created a vacuum, and other gangs have started trying to move into the area. Maybe they're targeting the Yacht Club."

"The Yacht Club is not a gang, Sheriff West. That's all rumor and innuendo, and I resent your implications."

Rebecca pulled her phone from her pocket and opened a browser window. "I'm not implying that the Yacht Club is a gang."

Chapman started to relax. "That's good to—"

"I'm stating a fact. Shall I read you the definition from Wikipedia? 'A gang is a group or society of associates, friends, or mem—'"

"That's quite enough. I don't need to be read to as if I'm a child."

"I thought perhaps you were unaware of the definition of the term. We know at least a few of your members have committed illegal acts, because I solved their murder cases, and I know what they did. Speaking of Yacht Club members, do you happen to know the whereabouts of Mitchell Longfellow? I know he's a close friend of Richmond Vale's, but he seems to be of no help in locating the man."

Chapman shifted his angry glare from Rebecca to Rhonda and seemed to be waiting for her to respond.

But the special agent simply stood there, her face completely neutral, and said nothing.

"I think it's time for both of you to leave," Chapman said finally. "Solve the case of my burned yacht or don't. I don't care. I, like so many of my fellow Shadow Island residents, will just have to deal with this unprecedented rise in crime without the help of local law enforcement. But I don't have time to deal with you anymore."

He gestured to the door. Rhonda's demeanor was obedient, even contrite, as she exited the room.

Rebecca stared at the back of Rhonda's head as she followed her out, new doubts about the agent's intentions swirling in her mind. Was Rhonda investigating their town on the orders of the Yacht Club? If so, she might know who was pulling the strings. Perhaps she shouldn't have been so quick to trust the special agent.

And if that was true, could she trust Jake Coffey after all?

17

Rebecca rubbed her temple, trying to stave off a forming headache. Rhonda's angry questions hadn't stopped since they'd gotten into the cruiser and only paused as they walked up the sidewalk. Once they were inside the sheriff's station, she started right back up again.

"I just don't understand why you had to go after him so hard. You can't know that the Yacht Club is even involved in this."

"If you think that was hard, Rhonda, I honestly don't know what to tell you. That was a polite and simple line of questioning."

"You accused him of being in a gang!"

"He *is* in a gang, Special Agent Lettinger." Rebecca walked through the bullpen and down the hall to her office. Once the door was closed behind them, she spun to face the woman she thought was a sensible, straightforward LEO. "The members of that gang are involved in a wide variety of crimes, from murder and drug running to shady land deals and witness intimidation. And those have just been since I took this job a few months ago. They've also bought innumerable politicians and officers of the law. I'd say that puts them right in gang-style territory."

"But it does mean they have better lawyers," Rhonda snapped back.

"As do all the big gangs! Need I remind you the Mafia is a gang?" Rebecca pointed between them. "We both know it. And you don't take a gang down by not asking questions or being afraid to talk to them when they're involved in a case."

"We don't know that he's involved in the case. We also don't know if the Yacht Club is involved in this."

Rebecca sighed and put her hands on her hips, dropping her head. She needed just a moment to pull herself together before she started yelling. She was so disappointed in Rhonda that it made it hard to think about anything else. "He *is* involved in this case because he's one of the victims, Special Agent Lettinger."

"He's also one of the big investors in town, Sheriff West." Rhonda put her hands on her hips now, too, and leaned forward. "And if you want to keep that title and keep investigating the Yacht Club to expose them for what you believe they are, maybe you shouldn't work so hard to get on his bad side."

Rebecca's jaw dropped. "What—"

"Yeah, you didn't think of that. Did you? Don't cut off your nose to spite your face, Rebecca. Sometimes, you have to play ball in order to do good at the end of the day."

"You don't get it." Rebecca shook her head. "You really don't get it. Rhonda, I don't want to be the sheriff of a town that's run by criminals and their lackies. I would rather give up my job here and move than do something like that."

The flash of surprise on Rhonda's face appeared genuine. "Are you serious? How are you supposed to take down the criminals if you're not the sheriff?"

Rebecca shrugged. "I can be a police officer in Lynnhaven or Coastal Ridge. I can be a private detective. I can get a job with the state police. I can work for insurance companies investigating fraud. Hell, I could go get a job waiting tables and still keep an eye on them and what they're doing. I'm telling you, you do not understand how blatant these people are. They think they own this island and everyone on it. We're not talking about a hidden conspiracy here."

Rhonda started to shake her head in denial, but Rebecca stopped her before she could say anything else.

"Walk out this door, talk to anyone on the streets. Hell, go down to a playground and ask a child. They know who the Yacht Club is and what they do. This is about collecting enough evidence on them to put them behind bars." She took a breath, licking her lips. "If you're going to investigate the rise in crime on Shadow Island, you'll uncover the Yacht Club if you only look."

"I did look. I didn't see how any of them were related to the Yacht Club."

Rebecca's anger receded as bone-deep sadness took its place. "Then you're either incompetent or you're wearing rose-colored glasses. Read the reports. Match the names. And I'll give you a clue. Anyone who's a member of the Seaview Marina is a member of the Yacht Club. That's their *gang* headquarters." Rebecca stepped to the side and around Rhonda. "Now if you'll excuse me, I have a crime to solve."

When she walked back into the bullpen, everyone was studiously working on their computers. There was no way her people hadn't heard at least part of that conversation, but everyone was doing their level best to stay professional and pretend they hadn't.

Even Hoyt didn't lift his gaze. There was a hint of a smile

on his face, however.

She kept her tone brusque and professional. "Frost, Darby, did you get statements from Ballard and Fairbank?"

"Yeah, Boss." Hoyt pointed at the whiteboard. "Both had alibis for the time of the fire. Fairbank was visiting his mother in a hospice facility, and Ballard was helping a friend move. We haven't double-checked those yet."

Viviane raised her hand until Rebecca pointed at her. "Ballard had insurance on his boat, but not enough to cover replacement. He also had a big contract planned that won't happen now, and he's going to have to refund deposits. This fire might bankrupt him."

"Well, if the fire was someone else's fault, he can always sue their insurance. Make a note of that for once the case is solved."

"Yeah, Boss." Viviane happily typed at her keys. In this job, it was always a blessing to be the bearer of good news for a change. "I got to tell you, though, Ballard has a wild temper. He was raging and whining and even buried his head in his desk while we were there talking to him. Frost wasn't even all that hard on him."

Rebecca hoped Rhonda could hear what was being said from where she was standing in the hall. "Did either of them identify anyone with a reason to burn their boats?"

Hoyt and Viviane shook their heads. Jake just kept pretending like he wasn't there at all as Rhonda finally joined them.

Rebecca ignored her. "Oswald Chapman claims his boat was there waiting for repairs and it was simply chance that led to it catching fire. Claims he has an alibi too. Was with Vale, discussing a new zoning ordinance. I'll be checking on that." She gestured to the board. "Bailey called me with the preliminary report."

"We saw." Jake pointed to the board where the report now hung next to the picture of the burn victim.

"As of right now, we don't have a name for him. No one's been reported missing either. But docks and boats are fluid things and so are the people who work there, so keep your ears open. Frost, Darby, go track down those two alibis if you can. Coffey, head down to the docks and talk with Dee Newton. He was also affected by all this. We already know where he was at the time of the fire, so focus on anyone who might want to put him out of business."

"You're going to check into the rest of the people involved and not just focus on Chapman because he's in what you call a gang?" Rhonda stared at the board, avoiding Rebecca's gaze.

"I'm not prone to walking around wearing blinders."

Viviane piped up. "Everyone is a suspect until they're cleared. That's what the sheriff's always saying."

Rhonda tilted her head as if conceding that point.

"You've all got your marching orders. Head out." Rebecca stepped aside.

There was a chorus of "yeah, Boss" and they all filed past. Viviane pointedly looked away from Rhonda as she passed, but Hoyt gave her a hard look. Jake, once again, moved like there was nothing wrong.

Rhonda waited for them to all file out before turning back to face Rebecca. "I notice that you made sure that you and only you will be the one checking Chapman's alibi. Is there a reason for that?"

Rebecca stared at her, feeling her face turn to stone. She couldn't believe Rhonda had the guts to question her like that. "Because I know this is going to be the most dangerous alibi to check out. Politically, professionally, and physically dangerous."

18

Sunset Suites looked like a decent place to Hoyt. It was designed to look more like a hotel than a hospital, except it still had that pervasive smell of antiseptic and cleaning solution. Considering they specialized in end-of-life care, the odor made sense. But it was still a depressing scent. He and Viviane were at the facility in Coastal Ridge to verify Cole Fairbank's claim that he'd been visiting his mother at the time of the fires.

Places like this always made Hoyt's thoughts shift to death and despair, and the empty waiting area reinforced the depressing atmosphere. It didn't matter that the place seemed clean and even luxurious—without any residents or visitors moving about, the mood was somber.

They sat and waited for the receptionist. There was a sign on the counter saying they would be right back. "Right back" seemed to mean something different here, as he and Viviane had been waiting for more than ten minutes already.

"Do you think Rhonda's on our side?" Viviane voiced the

main concern that had been zipping through his mind like a stubborn mosquito.

He shook his head. "I don't know."

"How could she be sent to investigate us and not know what's really going on in our town?"

"I don't know." He took his hat off and raked his hand through his hair before putting it back on.

"She was Jake's main reference. Do you think he's on her side or Rhonda's?" She continued saying out loud what he'd only dared to think.

He leaned back, looking down at her where she sat next to him. "I'm still hoping we're all on the same side."

Viviane nodded, clasping her hands together around her phone in her lap. "Me too. Mama and I didn't manage to learn much about who sent her down here. I'm still waiting to hear back from a buddy of mine that transferred to the Norfolk PD, though." She shifted in her seat before resting her head on the wall behind them. "This isn't at all like it was when Wallace ran the place."

"No. No, it isn't." Hoyt wanted to put his arm around her, to comfort her. More than anything, he wanted to tell her everything was going to be okay and that he'd make sure of it.

But he couldn't do that anymore. Even when she'd become an adult, Hoyt had always done his best to protect her. But now she was part of the team, and he had to treat her as such.

He took in Viviane's uniform, so new it still bore the sharp seams from the manufacturer. Glancing down at his own clothing, he noticed his seams were flat and honestly getting a bit worn. Still, it was the same uniform as hers. He couldn't disrespect her decision to stand shoulder to shoulder with him and take on lawbreakers. Once this training period was over, she'd be a full-fledged deputy the same as him. Same as Greg and Locke and Jake.

But please, God, don't let her end up like Darian.

Hoyt forced his thoughts away from the young deputy. "It's a lot harder now. The hours are longer. The cases are grimmer. We're no longer looking the other way." He swallowed hard. The image of three terrified little girls running out of an abandoned home and away from their kidnapper sprang to his mind. "If we'd been doing this before, maybe things wouldn't be so bad now."

"Mama also says that when the garbage can starts to stink, you have to take the lid off and wash it out. Jamming the lid on harder only makes the smell worse. Only soap and elbow grease will get rid of it." Viviane looked up at Hoyt. A lot of her innocence was gone. "I don't mind using some elbow grease and hard work to make my island a better place to live."

Hoyt smiled. Pride, shame, fear, and a healthy dose of paternal instincts swirled through him, making his eyes and nose prickle. He looked away and nodded. "Me neither."

"Doesn't mean you shouldn't wear gloves and maybe a gas mask, though." Viviane giggled.

He nodded, laughing away his conglomerate of emotions. "I've said it before, and I'll say it again, always use protection when you can."

"Rhonda wasn't right about one thing."

His laugh faded, but he kept smiling. "Which part? I heard a lot of things she wasn't right about."

Viviane sat forward, nodding her head to the side to indicate the blond woman walking up to the desk. "Playing nice. We both know hardball is the only way to deal with that group. They've been trying to get rid of her since she started. If they do manage to get rid of her, they're coming for you next. Then me, then Jake. She's just the front line in this fight."

Hoyt stood, ready to go speak to the attendant as she put the sign away. "Then we need to make sure we give her all the backup she needs."

Viviane shook her phone at him. "I already started."

He guessed she was referring to her earlier comment about having her mom look into Rhonda's appearance, but he had no time to ask about it as the woman in the white coat smiled at them.

Her name tag read *Susie*. "Who are you here to see?"

"You, actually. We're Deputies Hoyt Frost and Viviane Darby from the Shadow Island Sheriff's Office." Hoyt flashed his badge as the poor woman blanched. "I didn't mean to scare you. We need to follow up on a visitor who was here yesterday. He would've been in to see Marla Fairbank."

"Marla?" Susie spun around to pick up a clipboard resting on the counter and flip through it. Then she peered at them through oversize, square-rimmed glasses that dwarfed her features. "Yes, she had a visitor yesterday. Cole Fairbank. It says he was here at four fifty and stayed until seven fifteen."

"That's what the paper says." Viviane shrugged. They'd checked the log when they first came in and found no one around. "We need to verify that he was here. Do you have cameras?"

Susie put the clipboard back down. "No, I'm sorry, we don't. I mean we do, but they're not working." She leaned forward and lowered her voice. "We've got a leak in the ceiling, and it shorted them out. They're working on the roof now, but until that's fixed, we can't safely get the cameras functioning."

"And who was working the front desk when Cole Fairbank signed in and out?" Viviane used her brilliant smile on the woman.

She glanced at the pages on the clipboard. "That was Jared. Jared Pierce. But he's off today, and we're not permitted to give out personal information about staff or residents." When Viviane frowned, Susie was quick to continue. "I do, however, know that he usually works a second job when he isn't here. It's called Bean Tree Coffeehouse. I think it's out on that adorable island you all said you were from. I'm sure you must've heard of it."

Hoyt grinned from ear to ear. "Oh, don't worry. We know it. They make the best doughnuts in the state." He patted his belly. "Take our word for it. We're experts in that arena."

19

"Explain to me why we're stopping here?"

Rebecca was getting tired of Rhonda's incessant questioning. She wondered if she'd be pushing things too far to just leave the woman behind. Rhonda did have her own car, so it wasn't like she'd be trapped, and Rebecca could enjoy some peace and quiet in hers. She missed Hoyt's silent, reassuring presence. Mostly the silent part.

"Vale keeps ducking our calls so he won't have to talk to us. And this *is* an arson investigation." She waved her hand at the sign that read *Shadow Island Volunteer Fire Department* as she hopped out of the vehicle. "Seems like a good idea to talk to the people who were first on the scene and literally put out the fire. Plus, this is where the fire marshal said he was working today."

"He did?" Rhonda had to jog a bit to catch up with Rebecca as she approached the open bay doors. "When did he say that?"

"In the email he sent me this morning." There were only a few people in the garage working on cleaning equipment, so it was easy enough to spot the marshal. He was standing next to the wall, out of the way, as he talked to one of the men.

The marshal glanced up as Rebecca's shadow lengthened toward him in the early afternoon sun. "There you are, Sheriff. Thanks for coming down."

"No problem, Marshal Bentley, I know you're a busy man. And I wanted to say thanks to everyone who came out and helped us the other day too. You guys did hear that the Bean Tree Coffeehouse is handing out free doughnuts today to all emergency service personnel, right?"

That caught everyone's attention, and they all perked up and stared at the marshal. He sighed, and Rebecca bit her lip guiltily.

"I skipped lunch earlier. Do you mind if I..." The man Bentley had been talking to pointed out the door and started moving away, shooting Rebecca a smile while doing so.

She looked at Bentley and mouthed, *Sorry*.

"Fine. Go get your doughnuts. But you'd better bring me back some. Maple with bacon!"

"Yes, sir!"

Just like that, the building emptied. Marshal Bentley crossed his arms over his chest. "I was pretty much done with them anyway."

She smiled apologetically. "Oops."

Bentley chuckled. "I'd like to be mad, but I have to admit, I've already been by there once before coming over here." He rolled his eyes in ecstasy, his eyelashes fluttering. "Did you try their seasonal raspberry croissant?"

Rebecca gaped at him. "What? No. I didn't even hear about it. I love raspberries." The fire marshal seemed like a totally different person from the one she'd met at the scene. She supposed it kind of made sense. When she was working at an active scene with the lives of her people on the line, she wasn't exactly social either.

"You should go see if they have any. Even if not today, they said they'd have them until the start of November when the berries go out of season." He hefted the tablet he was holding. "But you're not here to discuss pastries. Let's talk pour patterns instead. Do you know what they are?"

"Only vaguely." Rebecca felt a little embarrassed to have to admit that. "It's some kind of mark left by the fire where it burned at a different temperature, and you can see the lines and splashes left by the accelerant that was used?"

"Close enough." Bentley turned so Rebecca could see the picture on his tablet. "You can see here, and here, what we call a 'wick, melt, and burn' pattern. This lets me know that gasoline was used to start this fire. Gas fires leave stronger patterns than other flammable liquids like alcohol or acetone."

"What about the marks here and here?" Rebecca pointed to the marks on the walls. They weren't as dark as the ones on the floor.

"That was most likely caused by a flashover fire created when the propane tank in the galley exploded." Bentley zoomed in on the burns, then scrolled the picture over to show the twisted metal, which was all that remained of what appeared to be an oven. "It was also what protected the body of the fire victim. When the door blew open, that metal shielded his body from the heat. I hear there was just enough left for the M.E. to get cause of death and find signs he was attacked first."

Rebecca nodded, fascinated by what he was explaining. "Then this was definitely arson?"

"Without a doubt. We also found some old life jackets which did not burn but were actually melted by the chemical reaction of having gasoline poured on them. They were above deck, closer to the bow. The fire didn't spread there." He flipped through to another picture. "Life jackets are made of closed-cell polyethylene, more commonly known as Styrofoam."

"Styrofoam?" Rebecca recalled a video from a few months prior, when she'd gone down a YouTube rabbit hole of questionable science experiments. "Gasoline turns Styrofoam into goo."

"A poor man's napalm, yes. I see that way too often in my job. Usually, it's just people being idiots and thinking that chemical reactions are fun without considering how quickly and easily a science experiment can get out of hand."

"And this was on the *Shoreline Catch*?" Rhonda had walked up a bit ago but had neither asked any questions nor tried to see the pictures. "Where the man was attacked and the body was found?"

Rebecca jumped in before the fire marshal could answer. "Fire Marshal Bentley, this is Special Agent Rhonda Lettinger of the state police."

Bentley gave the slightest acknowledgment with a tip of his head before answering Rebecca's question. "I don't know and can't say where the victim was attacked. Only that he ended up in the galley of the *Shoreline*. But we're not done searching yet. This kind of investigation takes time. We have to move slow so as not to compromise the evidence, which is already in a delicate state from the fire."

"Then how did the other boats catch on fire? Did they have any pour patterns?" Rebecca pulled out her notepad to cover everything she'd just learned.

"There are pour patterns on the other two. But not as large, and they could easily have been caused by something else. Spilled drinks, bottles that exploded in the heat...

there's a lot of flammable liquids that we use and store every day that most people never think about. Especially in kitchens, and all three ships had galleys."

Rebecca tried to understand. "Are you suggesting that something as innocent as a spilled drink or a kitchen ingredient could be responsible for this?"

He held his hands out in defeat. "We need more time to investigate that. Just like we need to check the dock itself, and I need to review the footage from the fireboats that responded to see how the fire reacted as it was being put out. Until then, I can't say one way or the other."

"We're in the same boat." She grinned at her own words. "No pun intended."

He chuckled, and Rebecca wondered if he was actually amused or just being polite.

Rhonda snapped open her notebook. "How likely would an arson case such as this be linked to owners trying to commit insurance fraud?"

Bentley frowned at Rhonda, giving her the same look he'd given Rebecca at the scene. "The number one cause of arson is teenage boys getting bored. Once you rule that out, it could be any number of things. Insurance fraud, covering up a crime, mental illness. If you want specific odds, you'd have to consult the GIS branch of the state police. They're usually pretty good at putting all those numbers together to figure out the statistics."

Rebecca hadn't told him in her introduction that Rhonda was in the GIS. She doubted it was an intentional dig at her professionalism, but rather an attempt to answer the question. Either way, it was a beautiful burn by the fire marshal.

And that pun was absolutely intended.

20

"I can't believe you're back for more doughnuts, Frost. How greedy can you get?" Vinnie, one of the managers at Bean Tree Coffeehouse, teased as they walked in for the second time that day. "Didn't you take a bag with you when you left?"

"I sure did, but this time, I'm here on officially official business, not just as a hungry guy who also happens to be a cop." Hoyt looked around, amused to see that the firefighters seemed to have finally gotten the memo and come down for their free doughnuts. He leaned against the counter. "Not that I would say no to another pastry if you offered one."

"Work first." Viviane shook her finger at him, then turned to Vinnie. "We were wondering if you have an employee by the name of Jared Pierce."

Vinnie's lips thinned. "I do...but what's this about? He in some kind of trouble?"

"Nope." Viviane shook her head briskly. "We just need him to verify some information for us. That's all. Is he working today?"

With a laugh, Vinnie waved his hand at the full lobby. "Everyone's working today. Jared's over at the case, setting out the latest batch. The guy with curly hair."

Viviane and Hoyt turned to look. A man in the teal *Bean Tree Coffeehouse* polo was standing at the case, a hairnet holding back his curly hair. He turned around and caught them staring.

His gaze jumped to their hats, then to the back of the shop.

Viviane flashed her megawatt smile. "Are you Jared? Can we ask you a few questions?"

"Depends." He half turned away from them. "About what? I don't want no trouble with the law."

"And we don't want any trouble with the man who makes our delicious food and beverages." Hoyt laughed, trying to put the kid at ease. Jared looked like he was going to bolt at any second. "You okay there?"

"I'm fine. I just...I don't like talking to cops." Jared once again twisted away as they took a few steps closer. "I had a run-in with some cops in North Carolina. I didn't do anything wrong, but it didn't end well for me."

"I'm real sorry to hear that." Viviane stepped out in front of Hoyt, and he let her. "There's assholes in every profession, but in some jobs, they can do harm to more people. Working at the Sunset Suites, I bet you know exactly what I'm talking about."

Jared nodded jerkily. "How do you know I work there?"

"Because that's why we're here. I promise we're not trying to pull anything on you. Just following up on a story we heard about a visitor that signed in Thursday evening."

"Who was it?"

"A man named Cole Fairbank. Do you know him?" With Viviane so calm in her demeanor, the kid was already starting to relax. He no longer looked like he was about to hurl.

"Marla's son, yeah. He stops by a few times a month to see his mom. She's having a real rough time recently, and he's upset he can't get in to see her more. But he says his job's always taking him away from the things that really matter. Seems like a nice guy."

"Did you see him last night?"

Jared paused, his eyes narrowing as he thought. "Yeah. I remember because it was near the end of my shift, which annoyed me. We have to walk the guests back to the rooms no matter how often they come in. That tacked on ten minutes, and I was almost late to my six o'clock shift here. Traffic is brutal on the bridge during that time."

"Awesome. Thanks, Jared. Have a nice day."

If Jared had barely made it here by six, there was no way Cole could've made it to the dock to start the fire around five thirty.

"Yeah, uh, you too. Was that all you needed from me?" He started edging away again.

Viviane laughed and waved him off. "That's all. Have a nice day."

Jared scurried off while Viviane and Hoyt turned for the door.

"Well, that's one suspect down."

Hoyt nodded and pushed the door open, leaving without getting another doughnut. That annoyed him, but he didn't want to freak out the kid anymore. Or his system with sugar overload. "Yeah, well, one down and a whole island left to go."

21

Hanging up the phone, Rebecca finished the notes she'd been jotting down. A heavy rustling at the door made her raise her head. Rhonda, carrying a box wider than she was, turned and twisted through the door.

Rebecca stood up, ready to offer help, but Rhonda shook her head. Then she dropped the box on the desk with a huff.

"You, uh, done with your phone calls?" Rhonda dropped into the guest chair closest to the door.

Rebecca raised an eyebrow and sank back into her chair again, checking her notes. "Yeah, Cole Fairbank's insurance agent was happy to supply us all the information I needed. Addison called months ago, shortly after the hurricane, to update their insurance information. They lowered their deductible to something more reasonable, raised the coverage amount, and detailed all the things that were on the boat in case of a total loss."

"Which is right out of the insurance coverage handbook they send out after a big event to try and get you to spend more money." Rhonda popped the top off the box, showing rows of well-worn folders.

"Exactly. The agent even said that Addison mostly went with what was recommended to her. He remembered because it was such an easy conversation. Addison didn't try to negotiate, just asked pertinent questions and supplied him with everything he needed. He said it was one of the 'easiest endorsements for an increase to an existing policy that he'd ever gone through.' And she did it for both of their boats."

Rhonda paused with one hand in the box. "Cole has more than one?"

"Yep. The second one is older and smaller, but almost as decked out as the one that burned."

"I don't remember a second boat from Frost's report." Rhonda dropped a handful of files onto her lap.

"It's in there. But they were worried they'd struggle to make ends meet with it since the second boat is much smaller and can't take the larger groups out." Rebecca wished Rhonda would let her handle the case and just focus on her reason for being there. "What's all this you've got here?" She thumped a finger against the box set on her desk.

"This is what you told me I should look into. Old cases from before your time. I'm going to look for patterns to the crimes he did try to file but were tossed out of court. There's a serious problem here if a county sheriff can't trust the chain of evidence to be handled properly. A bigger problem if he was right not to trust them. And a much, much bigger problem if I find names in common on all the cases that did get tossed."

A slither of worry wormed through Rebecca's stomach. "Well, you're going to find a lot of repeated names for the officer in charge. Before I took over there was only Hudson,

Locke, and Frost working." She tilted her head toward the box. "Their names along with Wallace's and possibly Greg Abner's are going to be all over those cases."

"Well, of course they are." Rhonda waved away her concern and sat back in her chair to start reading the first case file. "So long as they don't have any connection to the people they're arresting or the Yacht Club members who are involved, there shouldn't be any issue. But if all the cases that were tossed out for mismanaged evidence are from, say Frost for the sake of argument, that would indicate it's the officer collecting and filing the evidence and not anyone else."

"I'm not worried about Frost. The whole time we've worked together, he's never once seriously screwed up." She thought about the single fight she and the senior deputy had gotten into when she'd accused him of not taking his oath of office seriously. And how he'd admitted that he'd let Wallace take the lead in everything without asking any questions.

Rhonda lifted her gaze to Rebecca. "I'm still going to check."

"I didn't tell you not to. Just that I'm not worried." Rebecca stifled her irritation. "If he did screw anything up, I'll be able to razz him for it the rest of his life. So let me know if you find something juicy." She tried to go back to her work, but Rhonda kept staring at her, studying every expression on her face.

"Sometimes these crime waves happen because the local criminals think they have an in with the officer on duty. Which is why I also pulled up the work roster to match up with these cases." Rhonda shook a bundle of papers at Rebecca. "So I'll also be checking the time the crimes happened and not just when the investigation started."

Checking the time of the crime and comparing it to who had been on duty had never occurred to Rebecca. She'd been too focused on connecting the names of the criminals and solving the crimes. Rebecca nearly told her about Locke's past. But the man had sworn to her that he'd never done anything to help the Yacht Club, only talked about what he knew was happening on the job.

Locke was the weak link. If she could trust him, there shouldn't be anything to worry about with Rhonda poking her nose in everything.

"Don't forget that Wallace considered himself always on the clock." Rebecca opened her browser to look for any information she could find on Cole Fairbank or his second boat. "From what I've heard, the man practically slept here after his wife died."

"When was that?" Rhonda took a note on the work roster.

"I'm not sure, really. But you could always check the records." Something about Wallace's unfiled reports popped into her head. "Wallace was suspicious enough of the staties that he stopped filing reports after a while. He appears to have been spooked by one too many instances of evidence disappearing. You might want to add a cross-reference of the troopers in the area as well."

Rhonda frowned but added that to her notes. "That's going to make this even more complicated."

"If it was an easy pattern to see, I would've spotted it already." Rebecca sipped her coffee and kept her gaze locked on her screen. She'd found Cole Fairbank's social media page and was scrolling through the pictures, trying to get a feel for the life he'd been living in the months prior to the fire.

So far, there was nothing unusual. Mostly, it was pictures

of him out on his boat. By scrolling back two months, she found the name of his second boat, the *Reel Adventure*, and reached for her stack of sticky notes. Her hand hit the box instead.

"You know, Rhonda, there's a lounge in back. You could take this back there and be much more comfortable." She nudged the box toward Rhonda.

"Sheriff West, is there something you're trying to hide in your office?"

Rebecca scowled. That was both rude and stupid. "My patience is wearing thin, and I'm trying to cooperate while being civil. But since arriving here on your oversight mission, you have continually insulted me by not trusting me. Do I need to remind you what I went through on Little Quell Island to prove my level of commitment and integrity?"

"Do I need to remind you that I'm the one who got you off of Little Quell Island?" Rhonda countered.

At that, Rebecca took a steadying breath and tried to calm down before she said something she'd regret. "I have nothing to hide, and you of all people should know that, Special Agent Lettinger." She stood, picked up the box, and set it closer to Rhonda.

"And I am just trying to do my job—"

"And I'm trying to uncover my desk and all the things you buried under your box. If you insist on staying in here to work, at least move your crap so I have the space I need. Bring in the table from the lounge if you need more room, but I need my workspace back. Your investigation cannot hinder mine."

Rhonda grabbed the box before it could teeter off the edge while trying to keep the papers she'd laid out in her lap from spilling to the floor. "My apologies. I didn't mean to interfere or offend you. But it can't look to anyone like I'm conducting a biased review." She took the box and set it on the floor in front of her instead.

"Currently, you give the impression you're biased in favor of the Yacht Club." Rebecca shuffled some papers that had been buried under the agent's box.

She understood Rhonda had a job to do, but this felt bigger. The special agent's past behavior certainly never indicated she was in cahoots with the Yacht Club. But this sudden scrutiny seemed more like something Vale would pull.

Trying to ignore the hurt, she continued scrolling through Cole's limited social media posts. Two months ago, he'd posted a picture of himself and his wife having dinner at a fancy restaurant. It was the most recent picture of them. Rebecca checked the caption. "Celebrating news that Addison will soon begin her career in internet marketing and consulting!"

Next, she navigated to Addison's social media pages. Unlike her husband, Addison shared a variety of posts regularly. Her most recent one showed video of her standing before the Seaview Marina, captioned, *What a disaster! Our boat was destroyed in a dock fire.*

Rebecca's phone started ringing. The caller ID read Deborah Niece, and Rebecca smiled as she answered. "Hey, Deborah, how are you?" Deborah was the only remaining agent at the Shadow Homes Real Estate Agency since her best friend and business partner, Natalie Luptak, had been beheaded by a serial killer with a fetish for Lovecraft, elder gods, and leeches.

"Not great, Rebecca. Do you have a moment to talk, unofficially?"

That caught her attention. She and Deborah were

friendly but not really friends, so if this wasn't about sheriff business, she wasn't sure what it could be about. "Is this a personal call?"

"You could say that. 'Cause, honestly, I could get in a lot of trouble telling you this. But I can't in good conscience not tell you either."

Rebecca stood, Rhonda watching her every move. "Let me get somewhere private." She stepped into the hall, pulling her office door closed behind her. "Okay, what is it?"

"I got the strangest request today. It was an offer for the Sand Dollar Shores rental."

Rebecca was walking toward the interrogation room but stopped. That certainly wasn't what she'd expected. "I thought Mrs. Shuping wasn't going to sell the house after the tax thing was settled."

"She didn't list it. This was a request from a buyer, wondering if it was for sale. And with the type of money they're suggesting, I hate to say it, but Mrs. Shuping would be stupid to turn it down."

Rebecca's heart dropped at the thought of losing her cozy little home. Never being able to sit on that porch and watch the waves was not a worry she ever expected to have.

"And part of his offer is the insistence that the tenant, you, vacate the premises within thirty days of the sale."

"Well, can I counteroffer?"

"You could. I don't mean to question your net worth, but I don't think you could afford a bidding war with this guy. His offer is more than the inflated valuation from the tax scam a couple of months ago. Do you have that kind of money or credit?"

All her hopes went straight down the drain. "No, I don't have that kind of money. I have savings but not that much."

"Don't get too worried about it. I'll do my best to figure

out what's going on, then I'll reach out to you again. But I didn't want you to be blindsided."

Rebecca appreciated that and said so. If she was going to end up evicted, at least she'd have a chance to look for other accommodations now.

But as she reached her office door, this sudden turn of events only added to the eerie oddities enveloping the island. Was the timing of his development a mere coincidence?

Or another type of threat?

22

The house Viviane and Hoyt pulled up in front of still had the cheerful *Sold* sign on the post out front. There was a single car in the drive, and the windows were open. As they approached, Viviane saw through the screen door that the interior wooden front door was open. From inside, the sound of eighties power ballads and someone singing along blared their way.

They were at the home of Stan Harrod to verify Perry Ballard's alibi on the night of the boat fires down at Dee's Docks. Viviane looked at Hoyt, who indicated she should go ahead while he moved to the side. She pounded her knuckles against the doorframe, rattling it on its hinges.

A *thump* resounded from inside. The volume of the music dropped to a whisper as a man's voice rang out. "Hello? Who is it?"

"Deputies Viviane Darby and Hoyt Frost, sir." It still felt so good to use her official title. Viviane shifted away from the door as footsteps came closer.

The door swung open, revealing a man dressed in a tattered tank top and cargo shorts, his long hair pulled back in a low ponytail and his glasses sliding down his nose. "Can I help you? Was my music too loud? Did someone complain?"

"No complaints, sir. Are you Stan Harrod?" Viviane peered around him at the room filled with stacks of boxes. It was a complete mess. Some of them had already been opened then restacked so that the sides were collapsing.

"I am. Is there something I can help you with?" An even louder *thump*, then several smaller ones, trailed his question. "Ah, dammit. Come in, come in. I'm busy making a mess in here." He swung the door wider for Viviane to catch, then raced back inside.

Viviane cautiously followed him, looking around as she went. There was a couch, a kitchen table, and a coffee table all jammed into the front room, which was already piled high with boxes and bulging garbage bags. From what she could see, the rest of the house was bare.

"Sorry about the mess. Uh, watch your footing. My buddy and I just finished moving everything in late last night, so things are kind of piled all over the place." Stan was squatting down in the kitchen, picking up objects wrapped in brown paper that had toppled out of a box. Probably Stan had set the box down on the counter when Viviane had knocked, and it'd fallen to the floor.

"That's what we're here about. Who helped you move?" Viviane gave a passing glance into the boxes as she moved through the house. Primarily, she was making sure there wasn't something dangerous in them, but part of her was simply curious. One of the fun perks of being a deputy was getting to snoop without anyone judging her.

"You're here because I moved? Is there something wrong with the house?" He'd finished picking up the fallen contents and was inspecting them for damage before stopping to stare at them. "I paid for it fair and square. Went through an agent and everything."

"No, sir. It's not about the house. We're glad to have you on the island. But could you answer the question, please?"

He shrugged while still looking around confused. "Yeah, it was just my buddy Perry. Uh, Perry Ballard. We've been friends since we were kids. He's a good guy. Did we do something wrong?"

"Not that we're aware of. We're just checking his alibi for yesterday." Viviane watched his face, wondering how he'd react to that.

Stan chuckled, then shook his head, staring at the mug in his hands. "Oh, Perry, he's got a temper on him. But don't worry, his fuse is short. He'd never really do anything." He splayed his fingers out. "His explosions are tiny too. Stamping his feet, swearing a lot, that kind of thing. Either way, he couldn't have done anything yesterday, since he was with me."

Stan's view of Ballard matched her own, so that was reassuring. "What time was he with you?"

"Let's see." Stan put the mug on the counter. "He met me at my house in Coastal Ridge just after eight in the morning. We packed all day. Made multiple trips back and forth. Had lunch together, gas station sandwiches, before making one last trip over. He helped me unload everything and started some of the unpacking." He gestured to the chaos around them.

"And what time was that?"

"Around eight by the time we finished with the last load. But then we had to take the truck back to Coastal Ridge and pick up our cars. That was around eleven last night when we left my old house. He went home, and I came here."

Viviane looked back at Hoyt and saw he was writing it

all down. "And was anyone else with you when you were moving?"

"Not the whole time. But obviously we saw other people. The neighbors out here came to welcome me to the island. It's a nice, friendly place. But they did say something about bodies washing up on the shore recently...?" He gave them both looks, waiting for a response. "I think I read something about that in the newspaper."

"If you did, then you probably also saw that those were crimes that happened elsewhere, and we solved them." Viviane grinned, and he relaxed.

"That's good to know. This is my retirement. All I want to worry about is not running out of beer or bait."

Hoyt chuckled and tipped his hat. "Those are the best problems to worry about, when they're the only ones. You have a good day, Mr. Harrod."

Viviane rolled her eyes a bit at both of them. If this man was retired, then he was either really buff for his age or he'd planned his finances well. Or maybe driving cabs was a much less stressful job than being a deputy. "Again, welcome to the island. Be sure to give us a call if you need us." Outwardly, she beamed again, then turned and walked out the door, following Hoyt.

He was looking up and down the block and gave a wave to a little girl on her bike who was staring at them as if they were celebrities. "Two victims' alibis down, one to go."

"Is he really another victim? Oswald Chapman doesn't strike me as any kind of victim." Viviane was grinning toothily as she got into the driver's seat but couldn't help herself. She really wanted to bring down one of the Yacht Club goons that had tormented her island for so long. "How much do you want to bet that his alibi doesn't hold up?"

"No betting." Hoyt slid in and pulled his seat belt on, then turned to face her. "Is that the real question, though?"

Viviane chewed on that for a little bit before starting the engine. Putting aside her feelings, she looked at the case objectively as a whole and not just the part she'd worked on that day. "No, the real question is, was the fire the goal of whoever did this? Or did they kill that man and set the fire to hide the body?"

23

Rebecca was annoyed that Rhonda never moved her sprawl of paperwork into the lounge, instead seizing on Rebecca's suggestion by pulling the coffee table in and wedging it between the chairs and the far wall of the office. Rhonda played at interior decorating while Rebecca was trying to finish making her phone calls. All the banging and scraping of furniture across the floor had not made for pleasant background music.

She'd been forced to leave multiple messages for Richmond Vale, who had yet to respond to them. Now, at least, Rhonda was facing away from Rebecca's desk, stooped over the table and her paperwork.

Rebecca was researching fires and different types of accelerants, or at least she was trying to. This was a topic unfamiliar to her, and she had to keep taking notes while flipping back and forth between tabs as she educated herself—all while Rhonda muttered under her breath.

If the situation had been normal, Rebecca could've popped in her earbuds and let The Black Keys drown out everything else. Except every few minutes, Rhonda would have another question for her. Rebecca would have to stop what she was doing and answer her, then reply to any possible follow-up questions, before she could get back to her research.

"I can see why you were so gung ho about hiring additional deputies."

Once again, Rebecca looked up from what she was reading. "Yeah? Did you find something?"

"Lots of things." Rhonda flipped some papers back and forth before jotting down more notes.

Rebecca sighed. That was not at all insightful. "The extra manpower also means we can cover all the shifts without people working alone all the time. I really hate the idea of having one of my people out there without backup."

"The island is small enough. It only takes, like, twenty minutes to get anywhere. You guys could respond even from home." Rhonda kept flicking through papers without looking up.

"Less than five minutes to be choked to death. And it only takes a third of a second to pull a trigger." Rebecca stared at the back of Rhonda's head until the agent finally looked over. "Twenty minutes is the same as a lifetime when you look at it your way."

Rebecca swallowed the rest of what she wanted to say. But her memory would never let her forget that Rhonda, the state police, and the Coast Guard had been nearly ten minutes away when Rebecca and her people were ambushed. Not everyone survived that night. Rebecca herself nearly didn't.

She knew it wasn't Rhonda's fault. But in the back of her mind, where her nightmares did their best to destroy her sanity, she blamed Rhonda—not as much as the Yacht Club, but Rhonda should've been her backup, and she'd allowed herself to get distracted.

Keeping her words to herself meant little when Rebecca's expression spoke for her. Rhonda's face crumpled, and she opened her mouth to say something, but Rebecca's desk phone rang.

Saved by the bell, Rebecca twisted away to focus on her screen while she did her best to shove her dark thoughts down. "Sheriff West speaking. How can I help you?"

"West, how dare you go to Oswald's office."

Just when I thought my day couldn't get any brighter, Dick calls.

"Well, hello, Mr. Vale. It's—"

"Do you not understand that he's an esteemed member of our town? A man of great worth and power? You treated him like a criminal!"

Rebecca hit the speaker button and set the handset back in the cradle before setting her phone to record.

"He's not the kind of man who would set fire to his own boat! Every man, or woman for that matter, can accidentally start a fire. A candle knocked over, a pinched wire in the walls, maintenance done poorly. There are lots of ways a fire can start."

Rebecca held her hand up as Rhonda opened her mouth. Yes, they already knew the fire had been intentional, but Vale shouldn't have access to that information.

"And we're investigating every possibility."

He cooled down slightly. "The first two, I'll give you as a possibility, but he only ever gets his repairs done at the Seaview Marina, where the service is top notch."

Rebecca nearly did a celebratory fist pump. "Well, maybe you should tell Chapman that, since he told us his yacht was there because he wanted Ty at Dee's Dock to do his maintenance work before he left on a long trip."

Vale went silent for a bit, then came back hotter than ever. "I said repairs. And Oswald is free to take his boat to any mechanic he damn well wants."

"Of course he is. You're the one who said he only uses the one at Seaview Marina." Rebecca rested her chin on the back of her interlaced fingers and grinned at the phone. Pulling Dick's chain was a rare but joyful thing.

"Why are you even talking to him at all? He's the victim here. Not the criminal. You're supposed to be finding the person responsible."

Rhonda shot an incredulous look at the phone while mouthing, *What the hell is wrong with him?*

"That's for us to determine, not for you to dictate." Rebecca shrugged. "Tell me, Richmond Vale, where were you yesterday evening?"

"What? First you accuse Oswald, and now me?"

"Would you prefer we come down to your office and ask you in a more official capacity?" That really would make her day. She could make quite a production out of it too.

"I was...oh. I was having a late lunch meeting with Oswald." Sadly, it sounded like Vale was catching on. He was too shrewd to fall for her taunts or implicate himself in any way.

"And what time was that?" Even though she was recording, Rebecca still picked up her pen to take notes.

"We met at three and didn't finish talking until nearly seven. We ended up having dinner together as well."

Rebecca wrote down the times. "And where did you eat? Was anyone else with you?"

"There were some other people with us, yes. But just staff...no one important."

Rhonda rolled her eyes at that classist comment.

"And where was this?"

Vale cleared his throat. "It was on my yacht, the *Golden Apple*."

That goofy name knocked against Rebecca's brain—Chapman had said the same thing. "Was it docked, or did you take it out?"

"Docked."

"And where was it docked?"

There was another pause and a second throat-clearing. "At the Seaview Marina."

Rebecca wrote down everything. "So Chapman's alibi is, he was having dinner with you on the *Golden Apple* at the Seaview Marina, while the *Liquid Asset* burned down at Dee's Dock after a boat fire somehow reached across the water from the burning fishing boat that was moored in its usual place."

"Anchoring where you're not blocking the throughfare of any other ships is entirely legal in Virginia!" And Hothead Dick was back.

"I'm sorry, was that a yes or a no?" Rebecca loudly tapped her pen. "I need your answer so I can officially confirm Mr. Oswald Chapman's alibi."

"Yes."

Rebecca could almost hear the squeak of the word passing between the enamel, he forced it out through his teeth so hard.

"Thank you, Mr. Vale. We'll contact you if we need any further information." Rebecca tapped the button, ending the call.

Rhonda sat back in her chair and let out a heavy breath. "Are you trying to get on his bad side?"

Rebecca frowned and shook her head. "I'm convinced

the man doesn't have a good side, not unless you're made of money. Or are, in fact, money."

A pair of footsteps coming down the hallway caught her attention, and she turned to the door just as Hoyt came into view. "How did it go?"

He started to step into the office, then saw the mess Rhonda had made with the furniture. "Uh, well, both Perry Ballard and Cole Fairbank have solid alibis for the time. Fairbank was checked into a hospice facility in Coastal Ridge visiting his dying mother. Ballard was busy the entire day helping a friend move."

Viviane stepped into the doorway and took her time examining the room. "Damn, Rhonda, you're just straight up laying claim to Boss's office, aren't you?"

"What?" Rhonda looked around as if finally seeing the mess she'd made. "No, I was digging through some old files and needed space."

"I'm not sure if you noticed when you looted the table, but there's a whole other room just down the hall. It has couches, chairs, everything you'd need." Hoyt nodded toward the lounge.

Rhonda bit her lip. "I needed Rebecca's help to go through it all. There's a lot here, and it's pretty complicated."

Rebecca, ignoring the awkwardness, tapped on her phone to get their attention. Rhonda's witch hunt was slowing them down enough already.

"Chapman's alibi also checked out. He was having a long meeting with Richmond Vale on his yacht the *Golden Apple* at the Seaview Marina. And never taking Vale or Chapman at their word, Jake followed up with the staff working on the yacht during that time and they all stated that the two men were there. Of course, whether I believe *them*..."

Hoyt pulled his gaze away from Rhonda and her table of

papers. "Well, that's the three main ones. You want us to check into Dee and the other boat owners at the dock?"

"Not yet. We still have Serenity McCreedy's hoodie, and we don't know why she ran." Rebecca glanced at the clock. "It's about time for you guys to head home. On your way out, ask Jake to follow up with forensics on the chemical analysis. Then, in the morning, swing out and talk with the McCreedy family. Hopefully Serenity is there. I'm posting an APB on her. Maybe that will get her attention."

"Yeah, Boss." Hoyt gave one last look at Rhonda before he left. Viviane offered a dismissive sniff and followed.

Rebecca sighed and went through the steps to issue the BOLO before returning to her research. This was going to be a long week, even longer if Rhonda kept slowing them down.

Hopefully, whoever did this got what they wanted and don't plan to drop any more victims.

24

Rush hour was over. All the stupid little families were at home, sitting around their kitchen tables, sharing their days with their loved ones.

I sat in my car, staring at a house I could never afford, owned by a man I should've never agreed to meet. Yet here I was. Again. Just like last time, I was shaking, but it wasn't from nerves or stress like before. This time, rage consumed me.

My life was supposed to have gotten better. That was why I'd agreed to his terms. He had what I needed to make my life good and whole, so I could show the world I was worthy of something and that I wasn't just a pretty face. There was more to me than just that.

My whole body was tense. I wriggled my left hand, trying to shake off some anger. I couldn't relieve the tension in my right hand, however, as it was currently in my lap, clutching a revolver.

I wasn't a violent person, not normally. But when someone was about to destroy me, I would fight back. If lethal force was necessary to reclaim my life, so be it.

The first guy had been an unfortunate accident. If he'd just minded his own business and not gone where he wasn't wanted, he could've survived and everything would've gone according to plan. Then I wouldn't be parked here, waiting for the right opportunity to kill again.

This time, I would be getting rid of the man really to blame.

What happened on that boat wasn't my fault. I knocked the guy on the head so he wouldn't call for assistance. I needed the fire to destroy the boat, so I needed to stop him.

I'd tried to get him up the stairs to safety, but he was far too heavy for me. There was no way I could've gotten him up the ladder. And I certainly couldn't call anyone and ask for help. No, I was in this alone.

Story of my life.

Glancing up and down the street, I noted no one had driven by for at least ten minutes. The small, highly manicured yards were all empty and quiet. I got out of my car, holding the gun flat against my leg to hide it, and gently closed the driver's door.

If I'd done this instead of setting that fire, that innocent man would be alive right now. Balance had to be restored. I could make everything right again. Then things could fall into place just like they were supposed to.

Crossing the street, I did my best to slow my racing thoughts. It didn't matter who was at fault for that man's death. Arguments could be made either way.

As my feet hit the grass, I began to hear his voice coming from the backyard. All this money, the nice house, this swanky neighborhood, and he was an inconsiderate asshole who talked so loud in his backyard that he could be heard from the sidewalk.

Following close to the side of the house, I stepped softly,

keeping hidden among the pots of giant citronella grass that grew like a wall around the backyard. Tucking myself into the lemony smelling fronds, I peered through, searching for his whereabouts.

He was sitting in a chaise lounge with a robe over a tight pair of swim trunks. And like all low-class bastards, he had his legs sprawled wide open. His robe wasn't even tied closed. He held a phone up to his ear.

I looked around, just to be sure there were no witnesses. This had to be fast but not rushed. He didn't deserve to live, and I had to make sure I succeeded in ending him and his threat to me.

It was just him, sitting in barely anything like he was God's gift to women. The disgusting pig stared at his pool while a fire crackled in a chrome firepit beside him. An excessive and ridiculous show of wealth and stupidity.

He was distracted and clueless. Now was my chance.

All I had to do was raise the gun, aim for his chest, and pull the trigger. Surely, I'd hit something if I aimed for the middle. But rage overwhelmed me, and my hands began to shake again. I wouldn't hit anything if the gun was jumping around. I tried to breathe through it and aim at him, but my hands wouldn't obey.

Come on. Don't turn into a pussy now. This is the only way to be free of him.

Freedom. That was worth fighting for. Worth killing for.

I flexed my fingers around the handle of the gun and raised my arms.

A *thud* startled me, and I jerked my head around to look.

"You out back again? Why didn't you tell me? I would've brought my suit."

Hearing another man's voice, I shifted back farther, pressing myself against the wall next to the corner of the building. Green fronds filled in behind me, but not so thick I couldn't see. Richmond Vale walked past, stepping out through the sliding doors, and I nearly swallowed my tongue in shock.

It took me a moment before I could do anything. I turned back around, looking for my target. He was still in his chair, but now Vale was between us. I'd waited too long. I certainly couldn't kill him with an eyewitness standing there.

That was fine. I'd come back later. I had the rest of my life to make sure his ended. And next time, I wouldn't hesitate.

25

"Are you not hungry? That has to be a first."

Rebecca looked up from her plate to find Ryker staring at her. His plate was already empty while her meal was only half eaten. Granted, she had served him only half the portion she'd taken. His medication and headaches didn't allow him to eat too much in one sitting without feeling ill. That was yet another thing she worried about. How was he supposed to heal properly if he wasn't eating well?

"Not really. Today has been aggravating, and I'm just not in the mood."

He was right, though. It was unlike her not to be able to set aside work problems once she was home, at least long enough to eat when a meal was set in front of her. Tonight's was even one of her favorites, Angie Frost's cheesy noodles with crispy chicken and steamed carrots.

"How about we take this to the back deck, and you can tell me what's got you so twisted up?" Ryker picked up his plate and hers and set them by the sink.

Hearing the clinking of plates, Humphrey popped his head up from under the table where he'd been resting on her knee.

"What's that, boy? You want to go outside too?" Rebecca teased him, ruffling his head so his ears flopped.

Humphrey grinned up at her, his eyes squinted closed as he enjoyed the attention.

"How about you go get your ball, and we'll go outside?"

The dog's eyes shot open and darted around before he scrambled off to go find his favorite toy.

Rebecca laughed, watching him slide around on the slick floors before finding purchase on a rug.

"I should've known all you needed was his puppy antics to cheer you up." Ryker handed her a beer, and for a moment, she rested her head against his side. Solidarity or not, she was itching for an ice-cold beer, and he must've sensed it.

"Puppy antics are fun, but I think what I really need is to vent." Just saying that had her feeling better, and the tense muscles in her shoulders relaxed a tad.

Ryker took her free hand and helped her up as he called Humphrey. "C'mon, boy, time to go outside!"

They barely had time to open the back door before a ball-wielding lab streak bounded down the stairs onto the sand.

Ryker stopped as he stepped onto the back deck and looked around, confusion etched into his features. "Um, I know we came out here for a reason, babe, but I have no idea what it was."

"You don't remember?" Rebecca moved closer and peered up into his eyes. "It seemed like you were doing better with your memory. I mean, I know we've shared a laugh or two when you've used the wrong word when talking, but..."

"I think I'm letting myself get too worked up and the stress and anxiety are making the memory issues from the TBI worse. So did we just come out here to give Humphrey some exercise? That doesn't seem right."

Rebecca knew she should give him the time to try to recall the details on his own, but she needed to vent. "We came out here after dinner. We were going to talk. Do you remember what we were planning to talk about?"

Ryker glanced back inside as if mentally retracing his steps. His gaze drifted back onto the deck and the dog, and she could practically see the wheels turning as he tried to puzzle it together. Finally, his gaze darted back to Rebecca. "Were you going to complain about work?"

Rebecca kissed his cheek before dropping into one of the Adirondack chairs and leaning back. "This case is messy and awkward. I have no experience with arson and am having to teach myself all the nuances. Even taking pictures of the crime scene was the fire marshal's jurisdiction. I never even got to go onto the boat itself to examine the crime scene personally. I've been forced to rely on Marshal Bentley to give me everything."

Humphrey ran up and dropped the ball in her lap for her to throw.

Ryker waited for the dog to run off again before replying. "That sounds pretty annoying. And one of the boats belonged to Oswald Chapman, and it's part of the Yacht Club flotilla?"

Rebecca smiled, glad his memory seemed to be keeping up. She popped open the beer. "Yeah, the *Liquid Asset* was conveniently anchored right behind the boat that was the source of the fire, and where we found the body that we still don't have an ID for."

"Doesn't sound very convenient for Chapman." Ryker sipped at his drink while watching Humphrey nose around the sand, looking for his ball.

"Probably not. Which is why I have to keep in mind that this could be a targeted attack against either Chapman personally or against the Aqua Mafia."

Ryker nearly shot his drink out his nose and had to cough to clear his throat before he could talk. "The what?"

"The Aqua Mafia." Rebecca smirked. "The new guy dubbed them that, and now I can't stop thinking it. It makes them sound like little boys playing pirate lasers. I mean, it's an absurd name, but so is Yacht Club."

"Really? You think?"

"Yacht Club sounds like a boy band from the nineties or an offshoot of the Mickey Mouse Club."

Ryker shot his drink out his mouth that time, forcing him to wipe his face and dry his hands on his pants.

Rebecca laughed. "Anyway, having the Aqua Mafia involved in any case makes things more complicated. On top of that, I've got Special Agent Lettinger breathing down my neck, asking all kinds of questions. She's supposed to be here to investigate this 'crime wave' we're having, but all she's done so far is slow me down and make things more difficult."

"I thought you and Rhonda worked well together."

"We did. Do. Maybe." Rebecca gulped a few swigs of her beer. After eating so little for dinner, the warmth of the alcohol infused her stomach. "Truth be told, I didn't even realize it until today, but I kind of resent her. I blame her for Darian's death." They both took a moment to grieve the friend they'd lost.

Ryker had known Darian Hudson for years and only learned after waking up from his coma that he had died.

"Honestly, if you were in her position, with what appeared to be the cartel guys right in front of you, wouldn't you have stopped to arrest them too? That was the main goal, right?"

Rebecca shifted uneasily. "But I wouldn't have left *any* of my people just sitting out there. She had three boats. All blazing fast, all fully loaded with lights, troopers, and Coasties."

As if sensing her distress, Humphrey jumped back onto the deck and dropped his ball in her lap again. She twirled it around her fingers before throwing it for the lab.

After another contemplative moment, she continued. "It would not have slowed her down or hurt her in any way to send one of those boats out to pick us up. Instead, she left us there to die. If it hadn't been for you, we all would've died on that island. Even your injuries were because of her shitty management."

"There is that, yeah. Do you think that's why she's here?"

"What?" Rebecca threw the ball again, then turned to her boyfriend. "Like, to make amends or something? To get back in our good graces? So far, her visit hasn't felt anything like that. It's more like she doesn't trust me and is second-guessing everything I say or do."

He shrugged. "Maybe she's here to cover up her own screwup from that night."

Rebecca stared at him. That wasn't something she had thought of.

"What better way to make it look like she didn't do anything wrong than to discredit you professionally before you can make a complaint? Have you read the report yet? Do you know what she said about you in it?"

She shook her head. "No. Well, I've read the basics, but not anything Rhonda included. It was all too fresh when I got a copy, and I was simply trying to make sense of what was real and what I'd imagined or dreamed while unconscious."

"Maybe you should try to read it more thoroughly. That's the only way you'll know what she said." Ryker tilted his head toward her, holding her gaze. "It's possible that what she wrote in there is the reason she's here to 'investigate' you."

"I could check into that." Rebecca chewed over that idea, but it didn't feel right in her mind. Granted, nothing about Rhonda's visit had felt right, but it wouldn't hurt to cover all her bases either. Better to know now if Rhonda was working with or against her.

"But that's not the only thing bothering you, is it?" Ryker was giving her a knowing look.

Damn my inability to keep my emotions off my face!

Rebecca pushed herself upright. "No. Serenity McCreedy is back in town. I saw her at the dock after the fire was put out. She ran from me, and I don't know why."

"You think she had something to do with the fire? If this is all about the Yacht Club, then she'd be top of my list of possible suspects. Serenity's got a lot of anger. After what happened to her best friend, and then everything with Robert Leigh. It would make sense if she saw a chance to sabotage an...Aqua Mafia...member like Oswald. Hell, his boat probably hosted some of those parties. A little revenge that got out of hand?"

Again, that was a side of things Rebecca hadn't considered. "You're full of awfully good insight tonight."

Ryker laughed and gestured around them. "Heck, I'm just glad I'm remembering the long-term stuff. But when you're not allowed to do anything else, you have a lot of time to sit and think about things." He whistled for Humphrey, but the dog trotted up and dropped the ball in Rebecca's lap again. "Speaking of, have you heard back from Mrs. Shuping? Is she going to sell the rental to you?"

Rebecca groaned and dropped her head in her hand, only to get a wet nose to the forehead, reminding her to throw the ball. "And that's just one more thing. Turns out that Mrs. Shuping got an outrageous offer on the house already. For way more than I can afford."

"From who?" Ryker frowned, staring at her in disbelief.

"I have no idea. But if she's smart, and we both know she is when it comes to taking care of this house, she'll accept the offer."

"I can't believe she'd do that. After everything you've done for this island and its residents? She can't just treat you like you're a snowbird and kick you to the streets. Since settling in here, I've seen how much of yourself you put into this job. How much you sacrifice. I can't believe she'd go behind your back just to make some extra zucchini."

Rebecca snapped her gaze toward Ryker, wondering if he was messing with her or if he was having memory issues.

He cocked his head, seemingly unaware. "What?"

"Ryker, you said Mrs. Shuping was going to make extra zucchini."

"I did? Like zucchini bread?"

"No. I think you meant to say 'money.' Are you okay? Is this conversation upsetting you?"

He shrugged. "I thought I was okay. I don't even realize it when I do that. What was I saying...?" Ryker scrunched his eyebrows and focused on a spot on the horizon. Then recognition flashed across his face. "I was talking about Mrs.

Shuping not choosing money over you, since you're part of our community. Right?"

Rebecca took another swig of her beer, keeping a careful watch on Ryker. "Yeah, that's what we were talking about."

Maybe it was the low blood sugar from too many missed meals, or the depressive attributes of the alcohol, or even Rhonda's scrutiny of how she did her job, but right now, she wasn't feeling much like a part of this community at all.

26

Rebecca swung her fob at the half door and let herself into the bullpen, dropping her keys into her pocket.

"Hey, Boss, that you?" Hoyt called out from the back hallway. Both dispatchers had the weekends off since she'd set up a call service to cover them. Early Saturday mornings were normally a quiet time, so she was sure he was confused about who would be there before nine.

"Yeah, it's me. And don't give me any grief about never being out of the office. I decided to come in and see if I could get some work done on the case now that Rhonda isn't here to hassle me with all her questions."

Hoyt joined Viviane in the bullpen, both of them wearing their hats.

Rebecca sighed. "What happened now?"

"Uh." Viviane stared at Hoyt, then nudged him.

He frowned at her before turning to Rebecca. "Actually, we were just debating about whether we should call you."

"What is it?" Rebecca pulled her keys back out of her pocket.

"There was a call about a missing person." He passed a

notepad to her. "She's not sure if her husband is actually missing, or if he's just running late coming home from a charter fishing trip he was working."

Rebecca read the name of the caller and the address. "Give me a minute to listen to the recording." She walked back to her office, half hoping this could be related to their arson case and just as fervently wishing it was a simple case of a person who didn't make it home on time after a great fishing trip.

She walked into her office and reached for the phone without looking as she sat down. Her rear end hit the box of paperwork that Rhonda had moved to her chair. Rebecca grumbled to herself and stood up to shift it over.

Punching in the number for the service and then her code, she listened to the call.

It was a woman who identified herself as Paula MacDaniel. Her husband had not come home the night before, when he had said his ship would be coming in. He also had not been answering any calls or texts. She'd even waited an entire extra day, knowing sometimes things came up that could make him late, and she had learned not to worry. But today, he still wasn't answering and that was not like him.

The operator who took the call asked Paula if she'd called anyone else on the boat to see where they were. That was when Paula broke down and started crying so hard it was difficult to make out her next words.

"I-I heard about a body. They found a body at the docks, here in town. It's the one closest to our house. And... and I also heard they didn't know whose body it was because it was too badly burned. I'm afraid. I'm afraid if I call the captain of his charter that they'll tell me that's his body. That he wasn't late. Please, just...can you find my husband and tell me that it's not his body they found on the boat?"

The caller dissolved into incoherent sobbing then, and the operator tried to reassure her that deputies would be over shortly to help.

Rebecca hung up the phone and grabbed her keys, ignoring Rhonda's box for the time being. She walked back into the bullpen and found Viviane and Hoyt still waiting for her.

"Darby, can you comb through the statements from the people at the beach the night of the fire? See if we missed anything. Come on, Frost. Let's go find out what happened to Paula's husband."

27

"I hate these reports more than any other." Rebecca sighed and put her SUV in park outside the MacDaniel home. It was a quaint little house, with freshly painted storm shutters and a carefully maintained yard and garden. "When you're almost certain they're going to end in heartache and pain, but you have to walk in pretending that there's still a reason to hope."

"We don't know the body Bailey's been working on is Paula's husband's body."

Rebecca nodded. "Right. Especially since he was supposed to have come home last night. If that's true, he should have been out to sea Thursday evening."

Hoyt's eyes shifted to the side, and his tormented features suddenly smoothed into a professional smile. "She's looking out the window. We're on, Boss."

Rebecca did her best not to think of anything as she got out of the cruiser and walked up to the door. She didn't want her overly expressive face to give away her troubled thoughts. Paula MacDaniel had already broken down once. If they had any hope of the woman keeping it together long enough for them to get through this, Rebecca needed to be strong for her.

As they walked across the lawn, the front door swung open.

"It's him. Isn't it?" Paula clutched her hands together at her waist. "It can't be him. He wasn't supposed to be home until last night. Friday. Is it him?"

"Mrs. MacDaniel?" As the woman nodded, fresh tears pouring down her cheeks, Rebecca pulled out her notepad and discreetly activated her pen camera. "We don't know yet, ma'am. Can you tell me why you think the victim might be your husband if he wasn't due home until the day after the fire?"

"He was working a fishing charter. They were going for tuna. Sometimes that takes a while. You have to go out to the deeper waters for it. But he wasn't supposed to be home until last evening. So I'm really just overreacting, right? Because, like you said, the fire was Thursday evening?" She laughed a bit maniacally and bobbed her head repeatedly. "I'm just being silly. I shouldn't have called nine-one-one. I'm sorry. I'm sure my Mac will be home shortly."

Rebecca noticed a business card being twisted into a mangled mess between Paula's hands. "Well, we're here now. Why don't you tell us the name of the boat he was working on, and we'll call and see how they're doing? Or if they don't answer, we can send the Coast Guard out to check on them."

Or maybe Mac wasn't answering because he was in the morgue, at the bottom of the ocean, or living a double life. Instead of letting herself get distracted, she focused on any other possible outcomes, just like Paula was doing. Pushing her now would likely break her.

Mrs. McDaniel scoffed. "I've tried and tried to reach

them. I go straight to voicemail on my husband's phone, and no one is answering the work number."

"Is that unusual when they're out to sea?"

"Sometimes he works the docks for a day or two when he gets back. Cleaning or sorting things, moving things. You know. So he doesn't always come straight back. But he usually calls once he's back on land. Or...or sometimes, the boat drops off other crew members before him, depending on where the charter took them. Not all the deck hands call Shadow Island their home port. If they do that, then he can be late."

"That's also possible, yes. Why don't you get us the name of the boat he was on, and we'll check?" Rebecca pointed at the card in her hands. "Is that the name? Can I have it, please? And what's your husband's name?"

"Yes, I got it to give to you. It's in case of emergency. Maybe this isn't an emergency, though. I did try calling. I've called repeatedly, but I didn't get an answer. So maybe that's good news..." Paula held out the crumpled card. "My husband's name is Bolivar, but everyone just calls him Mac."

"We can sort that out for you." Rebecca took the card from Paula's hand and passed it to Hoyt. "My deputy will handle tracking down Mac. How about we go inside, and you can tell me more about your husband?"

Some of Paula's anxiety seemed to fade away as Hoyt took the card and headed back to the cruiser.

"Of course. I'm sorry. Please come in. It's so early. Would you like a cup of coffee? I'm a tea drinker myself."

"A cup of tea would be amazing right now. Thank you so much."

Given something to do, Paula turned and headed straight to the kitchen. "Do you like cream or sugar with yours? It's Earl Grey."

"Milk would be great." Milk in her tea was disgusting, but it was clear that Paula needed something to do so she wouldn't fall apart. Rebecca could swallow it and even smile as she did if it helped keep Paula calm.

The house was spotless, with homey little cushions on the couches and fluffy throw blankets on the chairs.

"Have a seat." Paula pulled out one of the kitchen chairs as she walked past. "The water's already hot, so it'll just need to steep." The woman moved around the kitchen, assembling dishes and rummaging through the fridge.

Rebecca sat in the offered chair and took everything in. Pictures of Paula and a man who had to be her husband decorated every wall. Some were of just the couple, draped on each other lovingly. Others showed them in big crowds or with a few other people.

As her gaze moved from framed picture to framed picture, she landed on a calendar. A giant heart was drawn around one of the dates in the middle of the month.

"Here you go." Paula set a cup with a mismatched saucer in front of Rebecca, along with a tiny metal cup on the side and a teeny spoon to stir the bland, unappealing tea. She added a miniature hourglass in front of the saucer. "And there's your tea timer."

"Thank you. This is so sweet of you. Can you tell me about your husband? You said he works the docks sometimes. Where does he work?"

"Oh, anywhere he can." Paula sat down, holding a giant mug of black tea. It was nearly as big as the cup Rebecca used for her morning coffee at home. "He's a hard worker. We both know how seasonal and temperamental boat and dock work can be, so, he likes to get his hours in when he can. That way, when there's nothing much to do, we still have plenty left over to live comfortably until the next payday."

Rebecca used that as an opening. "Has he ever worked at the Seaview Marina?" As the words came out of her mouth, she knew it was the wrong thing to ask.

Paula's face twisted, her spine hardened, and her shoulders shot back. "I said he was a hard worker, not a bootlicker or kiddie diddler. That's the only kind of people who work up at Seaview. Polished turds, all of them."

Rebecca blinked. She knew the Yacht Club members and the staff weren't exactly appreciated on the island, but she'd never heard someone speak out so strongly against them.

"I'm sorry. I really put my foot in my mouth that time. I was trying to think of the name of another dock on the island where he might have worked, and that one just popped into my head. As you can imagine, with me being both new and the sheriff here, that place is one of the few docks I've visited. None of the others seem to draw quite so many criminals to their waters."

"Oh, I'm sure. I heard about you going in there and ruffling their feathers. I've never heard of anyone doing that before." Paula relented slightly. "Most people are scared of them."

"I can understand that." Rebecca shrugged, swirling the teabag around to help it steep. "I'm scared of rabid animals and bedbugs, and the Yacht Club and their crew are in the same class as far as I'm concerned." That earned Rebecca the tiniest of smiles. "But at the end of the day, according to the law, they're people. Subject to the same rights and restrictions as the rest of us."

Whether it was having someone to talk to, venting her anger at the Yacht Club, or just the cup of hot tea, Paula was starting to calm down. The hands that had destroyed the business card were curled around the mug now, at ease.

"Mac and I don't have any kids. We wanted to save up money first so we could move off the island. Not far, but out of Shadow. We both grew up here. The stories about what goes on in the shadows here aren't just fish tales. I'm too old to have kids now, but we always talked about adopting and giving a child a nice home. We can't do that with the Yacht Club corrupting everything. Tell me the truth, was that fire somehow related to those savages?"

"Honestly, I'm not sure yet. The fire marshal is in charge of fire investigations. I have to wait for him to tell me what's what with the fire."

Paula's fingers tightened on her mug until they turned white. "So he'll be the one looking into whoever killed that man on the boat?"

Rebecca shook her head. "No, he'll learn how, when, and what started the fires on the boats. He'll know how the fire spread from boat to dock to water and to the other boats. Once he has all that information, he and I will work together to determine who's responsible for the victim." The last of the sand ran out of her timer, and Rebecca splashed the tiniest amount of milk into her cup to appease her hostess.

"I heard about the fire. And the body. I thought it was terribly sad, and I was just waiting to hear who it was so I could give my condolences to their family. Mac wasn't supposed to be home then. There was no reason for me to think it could be my own husband you'd found."

There was a gentle knock on the door.

Paula tensed. "Come in."

Rebecca turned to see Hoyt step inside. He took his hat off and faced Paula.

"Tell me the truth." Paula's hand dropped to the table, and Rebecca automatically reached out to lay hers on top.

"I was able to get in touch with the Coast Guard, who then radioed your husband's boat." He took a deep breath. "I'm sorry, ma'am, but the captain said they dropped Mac off at Dee's Docks on Thursday right after five p.m. Mac said he was planning to surprise you for your anniversary and was excited to get home."

Paula's fingers clamped onto Rebecca's, and she squeezed back, letting her know without a word that she was there for her. "Can you tell for certain if that body is my husband's?"

"We'll confirm it with a DNA analysis, if you have a toothbrush or hairbrush we could take." Rebecca was impressed by how well Paula was holding up under the disturbing news. "And if you could provide the name of his dentist, that would be helpful too."

"I have all those things." Squeezing Rebecca's hand one last time, Paula got up to fetch the items. "Just make sure you catch the bastard who did this to my husband. And make them pay."

"Yes, ma'am. That's the plan." Rebecca watched Paula disappear into the bathroom before turning to Hoyt, whose mouth turned down as he shoved his hat back onto his head. She knew he hated notifying next of kin, so she looked away to give him a moment.

Armed with a probable identity for their victim, all they needed now was confirmation. Then they'd have to find the person responsible for tearing this family apart.

28

"Aw, Sheriff West, you shouldn't have! You're always bringing me gifts, and the only things I ever give you are reports."

Rebecca grinned at Justin Drake's teasing. He was already set up and working at one of the tables in the forensic lab of Coastal Ridge. They'd been colleagues for a few months now, and she appreciated his attention to detail and the way he was always ready for another challenge.

"But you know how much I love those reports. They help me put away criminals, and that looks so impressive for my bosses."

Justin's grin faltered a little. "Wait, I didn't know sheriffs had bosses."

Hoyt laughed behind her as he found a stool to perch on. "They don't. That's her polite way of saying your gifts are almost useless." Apparently, Hoyt had become familiar enough with the forensic investigator to start giving him a hard time too.

"I'm my own boss. And trust me when I say my boss likes having her cases closed and with a nice layer of evidence to hand over to the commonwealth attorneys." Rebecca passed Justin the evidence bag they'd brought over. "I have some possible hair and saliva samples for you to test against our John Doe burn victim. Any chance you can move this to the front? His wife is going mad not knowing where her husband is, and she needs answers."

"Always happy to do my part to end someone else's misery." Justin nodded at the tray he was working on. "Just let me get this finished, and I'll start prepping it. You can set the bag right there."

Hoyt wheeled around so he could face Justin. "Did she tell you that her boss is also a harsh mistress who's making her work on her day off, even though she has two totally competent deputies who could've taken care of this for her?"

"She didn't need to, Frost. I could see that with my own eyes. By this point, I'm starting to wonder if she just sleeps in her cruiser, she works so much." Justin slyly glanced up at Rebecca. "Or maybe it's because her deputies aren't as competent as they believe they are, so she has to handle everything herself to make sure it gets done right."

"I'll go ahead and not answer either of those questions, as I'm afraid they might incriminate someone else." Rebecca leaned over to peer at the charred bit Justin was working on. "Is that for our case?"

"Sure is. Bailey managed to pick out some of the fabric from your John Doe. It had melted into his flesh, so now I'm attempting to separate them. She also found a cell phone with a SIM card, but they were burned beyond recovery."

"Well, I've got a possible cell phone number for you, in case you want to try calling it." Rebecca shrugged and tapped the paper that went along with the evidence bag. "Did you find anything else since she and I talked yesterday? I know he died of smoke inhalation."

"Honestly, not really." He set aside his tray and recorded his findings. "I don't think Bailey's in today. So we won't be getting any more samples from her."

"What about the purple hoodie? Did you find anything on that?" Rebecca stepped around him, noticing a bit of fuzz in a hue she recognized.

"No accelerants were on the material. Of course, that doesn't indicate conclusively whether this Serenity person wearing the hoodie did or did not commit the arson. Just that there's no accelerant where we assumed we would find some if she was the one to light it up." He pointed over his shoulder to where purple fabric was stuffed in a baggie.

"Looks like there's only one thing left for us to do." Rebecca turned around. "Come on, Frost. Let's get a warrant and convince Ms. McCreedy to talk to us."

29

Armed with a warrant, Hoyt and Rebecca approached the McCreedys's house and activated their pen cameras. As he made his way toward the front door, Rebecca walked up the path behind him. He saw movement through the cut glass windows in the door.

"Runner!"

Hoyt broke to the left while Rebecca took the right side of the home. By the time he reached the backyard, winded and sweating, his boss already had caught up to Serenity at the end of the yard and was cuffing her while reciting her Miranda rights. Serenity's face was red, her eyes burning with a combination of fear and hate.

The girl really was fast, Hoyt had to give her that. She'd nearly made it through the back gate before Rebecca caught up to her.

The sliding glass door to the back patio was already open, with Eustace McCreedy storming toward Sheriff West and his daughter.

Hoyt stepped in front of him. "I'm going to need you to stay back and not interfere with official business."

"What on earth do you think you're doing?" Eustace glared over Hoyt's shoulder as his voice grew menacing. "Why is my daughter in handcuffs?"

He needed to diffuse the angry father and try to get the answers they came for. Honestly, considering how little care Serenity's dad had shown for her in the past, Hoyt was somewhat baffled by his indignation. Maybe his concern was for his family name and not his daughter's well-being.

"Sir, we have a warrant for Serenity. She's been avoiding talking to us and she's a suspect in a murder and arson investigation. We tried to do this the nice way, but then Serenity decided to run." Eustace began to speak, but Hoyt patted the air to soothe the man. "Let's all go inside and have a chat. We can be civil about this. Serenity just needs to answer some questions."

In the sliding glass doorway, Kym, Serenity's stepmother, appeared. She surveyed the scene on the patio. "What's happened?"

Hoyt opened his mouth, but Rebecca stepped forward, keeping a tight grip on Serenity's hands cuffed behind her back. "Why don't we go inside? We can explain our presence and hopefully get the answers we came for."

They moved into the family room, the tension thickening as everyone traded looks.

Rebecca broke the silence. "Serenity, I'm going to uncuff you. If you run again, we'll be having this conversation in the interrogation room at the station. Do you understand?"

Ever flippant, the girl shrugged.

"I'm going to need you to verbalize your agreement."

"Yeah, fine. I won't run."

Rebecca unlocked the restraints and gestured for the girl to have a seat in a nearby armchair.

Kym perched on the edge of the couch, but everyone else remained standing around the room.

Clearing his throat, Hoyt nodded at the sheriff. Her ever-revealing expression told him she was doing everything she could to remain cordial after having given so much leeway to a suspect.

She inhaled before she explained. "Mr. and Mrs. McCreedy, I'm sure you've heard about the fire at Dee's Docks. Serenity was there that night, but she ran before I could get a witness statement from her. We've patiently been trying to get her statement about the events of that night, but she's resisted. I'm afraid we're going to need one now."

Hoyt noted that Serenity had tensed at the mention of the fire and seemed to shrink deeper into the leather chair.

"Why does she need to give a statement over some fire?" Eustace's slow crossing of his arms could've read as menacing as he glared at Rebecca.

"Sir, as I stated out back, it was more than just a fire. A man was killed. We need to gather as much evidence as possible, and that includes your daughter's testimony. I have to admit, her running from me, changing her clothes to hide her identity, and refusing to come forward makes it look suspicious. We can either have a conversation here, where she's more comfortable, or we can take her in for questioning."

There was no good nature or humor in Rebecca's smile anymore. His boss was showing her teeth, letting the threat hang heavy in the air.

"I won't allow it." Eustace shook his head. The streaks of gray in his hair caught the light. Those and his paternal protection were both new. No doubt nearly losing his daughter this summer brought about that shift.

From the confused look in Serenity's eyes, it was probably too late for his attempts at fatherly devotion. "She has nothing to do with that dock or anyone who was involved."

"Except we believe she might, because Oswald Chapman's yacht was also there and was caught in the fire. We still haven't figured out how the fire managed to spread to his boat." Rebecca turned that biting smile up a notch and took a step forward.

"Who's Oswald Chapman?" Kym was staring at them as if they were insane, her foot tapping silently against the thick carpet. "And what does he have to do with Serenity?"

If either Kym or Eustace were playing stupid, they were good at it.

Rebecca continued before Hoyt could answer. "A member of the Yacht Club and the owner of several payday-loan companies. Your daughter admitted she was involved with the Yacht Club, participated in their activities, and even helped with recruitment drives focused on minors. Now a Yacht Club member, Oswald Chapman, is involved in a murder and arson case where Serenity fled the scene and avoided law enforcement, all while trying to hide her identity."

"I didn't mean to!" Serenity's gaze darted between Rebecca and Hoyt.

Eustace threw his hand up, silencing her. "She was a minor when she made those mistakes. She's learned her lesson and is trying to move on now."

Hoyt cleared his throat, pulling everyone's attention to him except Rebecca's. "If that's true, then she should want to make things right and help us by answering a few questions about what she did. That's all we're here for."

"'Was.' You said Serenity *was* a minor."

Eustace narrowed his eyes as Rebecca repeated his words back at him. "So?"

"Past tense. Serenity, when was your birthday? Don't lie. I can always check your license information in the database, and I really don't want to have to haul you in for obstructing a criminal investigation."

Serenity lifted her chin, and Hoyt thought he saw a tiny spark start in her eyes. "September seventh."

"Which means you're no longer a minor, and you weren't when you fled from the scene of a crime and evaded police." Rebecca stepped closer to Serenity's chair and gestured. "Please come with me. We can either talk privately in your front yard without your parents, or I can take you in. Which would you prefer?"

"The yard. We can talk here." Serenity stood, and her stepmother began to protest. "No, guys, it's okay. I'll be fine."

Hoyt pondered if Eustace and Kym's actions were all part of an act to appear more caring about Serenity. Their behavior certainly didn't track with how they'd treated the young woman in the past.

"Mr. and Mrs. McCreedy, we can stay here." Hoyt sat in the leather armchair and gestured for Eustace to have a seat as well. He pulled out his notepad as he struggled to sort his thoughts, as he hadn't expected Serenity to run or Rebecca to go so hard. In the back of his head, Serenity was still the little girl desperate to be seen as worthy of love—a complex he was certain she'd developed from her father's constant absence. "Tell me something, where were you two on Thursday evening between the hours of five and six?"

"*Us?*" Kym clutched her husband's arm where he sat next to her. "Why are you asking about us?"

"Because if Serenity has a reason to hold a grudge against the Yacht Club and Oswald Chapman, then so do the two of you. Maybe you learned a thing or two from Robert Leigh, hmm?" Hoyt looked back and forth between the two of them. "So where were you? And can anyone verify it?" His pen hovered over his notepad.

Eustace stammered. "We...we were with Serenity. Having an early dinner."

Hoyt didn't even bother writing that down. "Five in the evening sounds like the normal time for dinner to me."

Kym shifted forward. "We left for the restaurant around four fifteen. That's what we would consider early. You can ask anyone at Selena's. The staff came out to sing happy birthday and give Serenity one of their famous brownie sundaes. I'm sure they'd remember us. The restaurant wasn't very crowded at that hour."

"I have to ask..." Hoyt pondered the parents sitting in front of him, who seemed to have such a different view of love for their child than he and Angie had for their two boys. "Why were you celebrating after her birthday?"

"Serenity's been very busy. Sometimes she comes back to the island and doesn't even bother stopping by." Kym appeared wounded by the girl's actions.

"Are you saying she couldn't find time to celebrate her birthday with her own parents?" Hoyt asked the question more ironically than anything. He knew adult children got busy with their lives and didn't always make time for their parents, even attentive, loving ones.

But they usually made time for free food and presents. In an effort to suppress his growing ire, he was open to hearing what they had to say on the subject.

Eustace's eyes betrayed the truth of Hoyt's words. The girl didn't choose to spend any of her free time with her father. "What we're saying is that Serenity told us she had other plans on her birthday...and before you ask, no, she didn't say what they were...and that she had planned on being on the island Thursday. So we planned to celebrate then because we didn't know when we'd see her again."

Hoyt's eyebrows quirked up. "Meaning?"

"Nothing sinister. I raised a strong, independent young woman who's very busy. We don't hear from her or see her very often, and we never know when we might see her next. That's all."

"Tell me more about the birthday dinner."

"It was the first evening I had free since I got back from my trip to Alberta, and as we said, Serenity mentioned she was going to be back on the island. Our schedules lined up, so we planned the dinner."

Hoyt dropped his head and counted to five the *one Mississippi* way. The anger he had for these people was too strong and he needed to dial it back. "After the year she's had, everything she's lost, the time she spent recovering, the nightmares she must have had, might still have... Why didn't you make more of an effort to support her?"

"Look, I don't need you to tell me how to raise my daughter—"

Hoyt leaned forward. "I'm asking where you were when a man was murdered and millions of dollars' worth of damage was done. It seems a little too convenient that you scheduled an early dinner just when the three of you needed an alibi."

Eustace's open mouth snapped shut.

Kym jumped to his defense. "No, we really were with her for her birthday dinner at Selena's. Serenity had plans on her actual birthday with her friends, so we celebrated when she and Eustace were both available."

"I'll just write that down, so I can add it to the official record, then." Hoyt jotted in his notepad while he watched

Eustace clench and unclench his fists out of the corner of his eye. "And what time did dinner end?"

Kym looked at her fuming husband, then shook her head. "Um, it was right around five, I think. Eustace and I were home in time to get ready to go out for drinks with our friends in Lynnhaven. Oh, that's right! Serenity called me and told me about the smoke she saw down by the water, and that she was going to check it out. She was worried someone could be in trouble."

"She didn't leave with you, then?" Hoyt kept writing, trying to ignore his distaste for these two so-called parents. If he just acted like a stenographer, maybe he wouldn't react like a father.

"Oh, no. She always goes for a jog after dinner. Says it helps with digestion. And she did have nearly half that brownie and several bites of the ice cream." Kym puffed out her cheeks to look fat. "She needed the exercise after that. Gotta keep that girlish figure to keep her boyfriend happy."

One Mississippi...two Mississippi...

"All right then, Mrs. McCreedy, after your stepdaughter ate a big birthday meal complete with an ice-cream-slathered brownie and then told you she was running toward a fire because she was worried that someone was in danger, what did you do?"

"I...went home to get ready for drinks with our friends, like I said. We didn't want to keep them waiting."

"I'm going to guess you don't really feel any animosity toward the Yacht Club members for what they did to Serenity."

Eustace jaw clenched. Maybe if Hoyt kept pushing, he could actually get this piece of shit to take a swing at him. Then anything he did would be covered under the law.

"No, of course we don't. Why would we? I know there

was drinking involved, but it was in international waters, so it was all legal. And Serenity has always been wise beyond her years. She's such an independent girl." Eustace folded his arms again, satisfied with his explanation.

"Girl." Hoyt jammed the notepad and pen into his pocket, checking the top of the pen to make sure it was still recording. "That's the pertinent word here."

Kym shook her head in confusion. "What?"

"*Girl*, a female *child*. A child. She was a child. And you let her go off into international waters with strange men who only wanted her because of the way she looked. You knew they were giving her alcohol. You could assume they were giving her drugs. Which means you knew what they were doing with her. *To* her. Convincing her to do with them."

"Oh, come on." Eustace threw up his hands. "She wanted to go to those parties. And her grades never dipped. She would've hated us if we made her stop going."

Hoyt gripped the arms of the chair to keep his hands to himself. "Children need limits set by their parents. When they have no guidance, they become easy prey for people with bad intentions. Since you've absolved yourself of guilt, now the only people Serenity has to hate are herself and them. Because you left her all alone."

30

"You're a smart kid, Serenity." Rebecca turned to her as soon as they reached the grass. After months of concern, she was worried the child victim had turned into an adult criminal. "Tell me what happened Thursday evening. Starting at four."

Serenity jammed her hands in her back pockets and twisted back and forth. Rebecca realized she was scanning the area, probably to make sure no one else could hear her. Was it because she was embarrassed, or was she worried about the danger created by talking to the police? Or maybe she was concerned her earlier stunt still had nosy neighbors eyeing the house.

The girl's best friend had been killed because of Yacht Club machinations. And Serenity had been in with that group for a lot longer and gotten deeper too. She'd probably seen enough to know how violent they could be and could offer some details that might help put them behind bars.

"We can go down to the station if you want. No one has to know you spoke to me or what you said."

Serenity turned back, her gaze searching Rebecca's face.

Whatever she saw there must have put her more at ease because she finally started talking.

"I was here at four," she gestured toward the house, "messing around on my phone and checking social media. I left Chris last week when I signed the contract with Bay Belles modeling in New York City. My new apartment there isn't vacant yet, so I'm hanging out here until I can leave. It's cheaper than staying at the Sunrise Cove Motel. Besides, the owner of that place gives me the creeps. I knew with my dad always traveling that I could chill here and be left alone. Except, of course, when Kym tries to drag me shopping with her like we're best friends or something."

That sounded so flat and straightforward, Rebecca didn't doubt a word of it. That wouldn't stop her from double-checking later, though.

"We went to dinner at Selena's around four fifteen. Dad and Kym had plans to grab drinks with friends of theirs later, so we went early. Honestly, I prefer it when they're away, so I didn't really mind. We all drove together. We had dinner, and then Kym told the server it was my birthday. She wanted to make a big deal out of it. It's pretty lame when the servers all stand around you and sing as loud as they can anyway."

Rebecca groaned in sympathy. "Very lame."

Serenity laughed before continuing. "Honestly, I think Kym was way more into it. I played along and ordered their brownie à la mode while they had cocktails." She glanced at the front door, her smile vanishing as quickly as it had appeared. "That was their second round. I didn't feel comfortable riding with them after they'd been drinking, so I told them I wanted a jog after dinner and would run home."

"And after that?" Rebecca went back to her notes.

"About halfway here, I saw the smoke. Dad didn't pick up when I called him, so I called Kym. She didn't think it was a big deal, but I told her to call nine-one-one anyway. I got worried someone might be in trouble, so I ran toward the smoke. A firefighting boat was already there. There wasn't much I could do, so I just kind of stood around. I know how it sounds, but the fire was kind of mesmerizing. Not in a good way, just, I couldn't stop watching it."

Rebecca wrote a note to check the 911 call log to see if Kym ever made that call. "It can be, yeah. But why did you run from me when I called for you to stop?"

She tried to think back and remember if she'd seen a purple hoodie anywhere at the scene before they'd started taking witness statements. Her pen-camera footage hadn't shown Serenity was there, but it was possible she'd hung around the back of the crowd.

The fire had been so bright along with the near-blinding floodlights, Rebecca felt sure she'd have noticed Serenity's purple hoodie if she'd been there earlier.

The young woman shrugged, shoving her hands deeper into her pockets. "I ran because...I was scared."

"Scared of what?" That sounded like an excuse.

"You."

"Me?" Rebecca was genuinely surprised. "Why? If you did nothing wrong, didn't break any laws, then why would you be afraid of me?"

Even as she asked the question, Rebecca had a good idea why Serenity would be distrustful. She'd had to ask hard questions when Serenity's best friend died. And the young woman had next to no reason to respect any adult.

"Because...I don't know. I just was. I wasn't thinking." Serenity yanked her hands free and crossed her arms. "You yelled at me, and I just had to get out of there. I was so scared. I felt like I couldn't breathe." Her hand fluttered up to her neck while the other clutched her elbow.

"And...?" Rebecca prompted.

"Look, it's dumb. I know it's dumb. But to be honest, Sheriff West, you scare the shit out of me. I know you saved my life. I know I should, like, worship you as a hero or whatever. But I don't. Okay? I don't. I'm thrilled you saved me, and I'm grateful."

"But?"

Serenity was shifting her weight from one foot to the other and back again, a nervous movement. "But every damn time I close my eyes, it's not Owen I see as the life is choked out of me. It's you. It's your voice I hear when I can't breathe. And I don't even know what you're saying. I barely even remember what happened to me. The only reason I even know your voice is because you called me so many times after that."

Tears built in Serenity's eyes and trickled down her cheeks.

Rebecca's heart softened. It didn't sound like Serenity was lying. She sounded deeply troubled. "Then why did you ditch your hoodie behind Second Place?"

"Because..." Serenity's eyes unfocused as her eyebrow twitched slightly. "It was dirty. I had to get it off. I couldn't shower fast enough to try to feel clean again."

"Do you know Cole Fairbank?"

Serenity shook her head.

"Do you know Perry Ballard?"

The skin under Serenity's eye pulsed, and she started to shake her head, then stopped. "Maybe. His name sounds familiar."

"He runs Look Around and does whale-watching and dolphin-viewing cruises."

Serenity brightened a bit and the twitch under her eye stopped. "The dolphin guy, yeah. My mom took us out on one of his cruises when I was a kid."

"That must have been more than ten years ago." In Rebecca's research into how to help Serenity, she'd looked into what kind of support system she had at home and learned about her mother's death in a boating accident. She jotted a note to herself to see if any of the boats docked at Dee's had been involved with that.

"Well, it's one of the few memories I have with my mom, so I remember it well. She wore a red tank top that shimmered and a pair of cream-colored shorts. We sat at the rail and giggled together when the water splashed us. It was a great trip. And Captain Ballard told the silliest stories the whole time too." Serenity's lips pulled back into the saddest mimicry of a smile. "Those were good times."

That made Rebecca sigh. She knew that feeling all too well. When your fondest moments with your beloved parents turned bittersweet after they died. "You said you called your stepmom when you saw the smoke. Do you know what time that was?"

Serenity pulled her phone out of her pocket and pressed a few keys. "It was five forty-two." She turned the phone around so Rebecca could see the screen.

Rebecca wrote that down. "Thanks."

Serenity toggled a few more keys. "And dinner ended at five twenty-seven 'cause that's when I paid the bill." Once again, she showed her screen. It was a cash app transfer for thirty dollars sent to Orson McCreedy.

"Can you send me those? Or will you give me permission to access your bank and phone records?" Rebecca bit her tongue on the comment she wanted to make about a daughter reimbursing her father for her own birthday dinner.

"Yeah, what's your email? I'll send them right over." When Rebecca recited her email, Serenity punched it into her phone before putting the device away again. Then she resumed fidgeting and scanning the area.

Rebecca pulled her wallet, plucked a business card out, and wrote on the back of it. "The reason I called you so many times after what happened was because I wanted to get you the proper help you'd need to deal with the trauma you went through. What you're experiencing now is likely caused by that." She handed the card to Serenity, who handled it like she was afraid it would bite.

"I'm fine."

"Listen, those services are still available to you. On that card, I wrote the number for the Virginia Victim's Resources group. The second number is for Deputy Darby. If you ever need to talk to one of us, and it's too difficult to talk to me, you can always talk to her. Or any of the other deputies on staff. We're here to help you. You're part of our community, and we all swore oaths to help keep you safe."

Rebecca didn't take it personally when Serenity handled the card more easily once she heard Viviane's name.

The front door slammed, and Serenity jumped and stared guiltily at it. Hoyt stormed out of the house and made a wide berth around them.

"That's Deputy Frost, in case you didn't know. You can call him anytime too. He'd be more than happy to help you."

Help you kick your parents' asses from the look of him.

"Thank you. But like I said, I'm moving to New York soon." With one final check for anyone eavesdropping or spying on them, Serenity tucked the card into her pocket.

"Which is fine. Phones still work there. Or text messages.

Whatever you prefer." Rebecca took a step away, and Serenity started to relax for the first time since she'd seen her at the docks. "Call if you need anything. And next time I need something from you, I'll make sure to send one of the others if you need someone to talk to."

"Thank you. Not just for saving my life, you know, before." Tears welled in the young woman's eyes again. "But for believing me now."

Rebecca smiled, nodded, and turned to get in the SUV with her deputy. She didn't have it in her to tell the young woman that she'd be double-checking everything.

Trust but verify, as Dad used to say.

31

Rebecca didn't know what had happened between Hoyt and the McCreedy parents. Whatever it was, it kept him steaming mad the entire way back to the station. She'd been on the phone for the ride back, so she hadn't had a chance to ask him. He was still fuming when they walked into the bullpen, and he collapsed at his desk.

Viviane watched with concerned eyes. "Did it go badly?"

Rebecca shrugged noncommittally. "I don't know how it went with the parents, but I did learn that Serenity has a fairly solid alibi for the time the fire was set. She was alone, jogging, but on the phone with her stepmother, asking for help and advice, which she did not get. Serenity claims she ran toward the fire to see if anyone needed help and didn't get there until it was already being handled."

"And what do you think?"

"Considering I didn't see her until then, I'm inclined to believe her. Can you reach out to the witnesses and ask them if they saw Serenity or a figure wearing a purple hoodie? Also double-check with dispatch to see if Kym McCreedy ever bothered to call."

"Can do, Boss."

"That's about the same story I got from the parents as well." Hoyt pulled his hat off and ran his thumb over the emblem stitched to it. "They claimed Serenity was celebrating her birthday with her friends. And they're probably telling the truth. But they have so little regard for her or her safety, I nearly lost it on them. She has no support system, not from those people. I'd love to charge those assholes with child abandonment."

"They didn't buy her dinner. She had to pay for it herself." Rebecca rotated her neck, understanding that Hoyt's fatherly protective side was showing. She needed to focus less on how terrible Serenity's parents were and more on what was relevant to the case. "I asked her why she ran from me that night and learned she's still traumatized from the incident with Owen Miller. Apparently, she's had no support or therapy to deal with what happened to her in June."

Hoyt clenched his jaw. "After nearly being killed? Didn't you give her parents all the victim services contact information?"

"I did. Because by then, Serenity had already run back to Norfolk, and she wasn't answering my calls or returning my messages. When I called her stepmother, she said she'd pass on the information and make sure Serenity was okay."

"What the hell is wrong with those people?" Viviane spoke in little more than a whisper as she stared at Rebecca and Hoyt.

"No clue. But they don't deserve kids." Hoyt tossed his hat on his desk. "But that rules Serenity out as a likely suspect. Vi, I'll help you go through the list of witnesses."

Rebecca walked to the board and wrote out the update under Serenity's name, which they'd already linked to the picture of the hoodie. She also wrote the name of the modeling agency Serenity said she'd signed with.

"That's the last name off our list. The owners of the boats and Serenity have alibis. It's time to cast a wider net for the list of possible suspects. We can't forget that the dock itself was also damaged. This could've been all about Dee Newton."

"We already asked him if he had any enemies." Viviane looked over at Hoyt, and he nodded in agreement.

She'd been doing that a lot more recently, and it was starting to worry Rebecca that Viviane kept checking with the others. Lack of self-assurance. Rebecca made a mental note to keep an eye out for that. "But we haven't checked into his relationship with Ballard or Fairbank."

"We also didn't check his insurance coverage or the condition of the dock." Hoyt got up to make himself a cup of coffee, looking much calmer now. "Having a boat catch fire while tied down could end up being a big payout for Dee. He'll get the dock repair covered by his insurance company that'll turn around and sue the owner of the boat where the fire started if he's found at fault."

"Do you really think he'd do something like that?" Viviane seemed shocked at the idea. "What about the body on the boat?"

Rebecca shrugged. "Paula MacDaniel said her husband Mac was a dock worker. Maybe he picked up a gig at Dee's. A little quick arson that got out of control, and he ended up knocked out somehow and died. The fire marshal said most arsonists end up becoming their own victims. And people can do extreme things when they think there's an easy way to make money."

Hoyt grunted into his coffee cup. "That's an angle I

hadn't thought of yet. That the victim could also be the perp."

"Or that Dee could have something to do with it. Just because we knew where he was when the fire started..." Viviane pursed her lips. "I suppose it could even be possible that he set the fire small, somehow, then left to make sure he had an alibi for when it reached the gasoline or something."

Drawing a circle around the picture of the corpse, Rebecca tapped it. "We don't have a solid ID for him yet, but we do have a likely one. Let's go ahead and dig into Bolivar 'Mac' MacDaniel. I don't want to take this to his wife yet, so get creative. Talk to people who might've worked with him at the docks and on the charter boats. I'm going to try to meet up with Fire Marshal Bentley."

32

The parking lot of Dee's Dock was half full, the road completely empty as I came around the last curve. Everyone was already where they needed to be. Most of the cars in the lot had official government plates, meaning the police and all their minions were there.

Which was a good thing for me, since I needed to try to gauge if the cops were close to figuring out this was all my fault. But I had to do it without being seen. Though if push came to shove, I could always just say I was curious as to how things were going.

Oh god, why didn't I come up with a better excuse? I could've brought a bucket and pretended to be oyster hunting around the docks. It was always a good place to find the really briny ones.

Maybe I should try that instead? No. No one would be eating any shellfish from this area after all that gasoline and oil I spilled into the water. All I could do was try my best to look like I wasn't guilty. Just another rubbernecker, here to see what all the fuss was about. It was natural to be captivated by these things.

Don't mind me, everyone.

At least I had a decent angle on the docks from here, and the parked cars gave me good cover.

The voices of the people on the docks echoed up from the water, but it wasn't easy to make out the words. I thought I heard "sheriff" and risked a glance. Sheriff West, with her signature blond ponytail swaying, had just reached the bottom of the ramp and was greeting a man the others seemed to be taking orders from. He must've been the fire marshal the volunteer fire department people had talked about.

I moved closer, slowing my breathing so I could hear him speak.

"No, there are no signs that accelerant was added to the dock, but the ropes melted away, so we couldn't check those. From the looks of it, the fishing boat had the most distinct pour marks."

It sounded like he cleared his throat before he continued. "The results from the corpse's clothing came in. He didn't have any accelerant poured on him either. With that in mind, I'd guess that his death wasn't the main objective. Killers tend to focus on their victims."

They knew about the oil. They knew where I'd started the fire. And they even guessed I didn't mean to kill that guy.

"Bolivar MacDaniel."

I froze at Sheriff West's words. I knew that name. At least, I'd heard it before.

"Is that the name of the victim?"

I held my breath, waiting for the sheriff to answer the marshal.

"We think so. The DNA analysis is being expedited. You saw what was left of him. And we've got no hits for dental records."

I nearly puked and had to swallow it back down. I'd done that. That was my fault. My knees gave out, and I fell into the sandy mix of gravel, my back arching as my stomach churned. I clamped my teeth together, holding in the pain that staggered me. What had I become?

A killer.

Ice slid down my spine, and my body stilled. The burning sensation in my throat faded. It was the same way I felt when I'd first talked to the deputies. But it had worked then. They had believed everything I'd said. My ears stopped ringing, and I could hear the fire marshal talking.

"If the fire hadn't been put out, the tank could've exploded. Thankfully, the water cannon focused on the fuel tanks, and the source was snuffed before that happened. Oil was poured into the water as well. That's what caught the yacht on fire. It was the puddle in the water that lit the dock, which exacerbated the blaze because the wood created a steady-burning fuel source, so the fire consumed more than its initial target. The dock was probably in pretty good condition beforehand, considering how much of it is still intact."

Oh, thank god. They hadn't pieced it together.

I was directed to pour oil on the yacht. But when the deckhand had come onto my boat, I'd had to knock him out. Then I wasted too much time trying to lift him and drag him out of the galley and didn't have time to douse the yacht in oil. Instead, I'd lit the oil container and tossed it over the railing of the *Shoreline Catch*, hoping it would reach the yacht. And it worked.

Though I might not have followed his instructions exactly, the end result was the same. Both of our boats had burned.

I might've been the one who started the fire, but he was the one calling the shots. This was his fault. It wasn't mine.

Walking casually, I retreated through the parking lot. As soon as my feet hit the grass, I scurried away as quickly as I dared without drawing unnecessary attention.

I had to make this right.

No.

I had to make this stop.

That would make everything right again.

I hoped.

33

Back at the station, Rebecca relayed to Viviane and Hoyt everything she'd learned from her outing at the dock with Marshal Bentley. Once again, they had to change the way they looked at the case. At least now they could focus on the real target...whoever that might be.

"Which means the *Shoreline Catch* was the original target of the arsonist's fire?" Hoyt twisted back and forth in his seat, frowning at the board.

"That's what the science is telling us. In fact, Mac could've been a victim of chance. Marshal Bentley said there was no gasoline found on him." Rebecca slid the pictures of the *Liquid Asset* and the *Look Around* off to one side.

"You mean the poor guy just happened to be in the wrong place at the wrong time, got smashed in the head, and ended up dying in the fire by chance?" Viviane looked horrified.

Personally, Rebecca thought it would be worse if someone had planned to kill him that way, but she could see Viviane's point of view too.

"What about the dock itself? Is Dee out of the running

for psycho of the year then?" Hoyt grinned at his own dark joke.

"The dock was in good condition. In fact, it's the reason the fire didn't spread farther. The wood was solid and coated in fire retardant, and the fire safety supplies exceeded what's required for a dock that size. Unless we can find a reason Dee had it in for Cole Fairbank, I can't come up with any motive for his having set the fire."

"You want us to change the direction of our investigation to focus on Fairbank, then?"

"The Fairbanks, both of them." Rebecca added Addison's name to the board. "She was the one in charge of the money. And she was the one who upped the insurance coverage. We need to learn what she was doing that day too."

"Oh, I know!" Viviane perked up and started typing on the computer, then leaned over to turn on her speakers.

Addison's voice filled the station. *"Greetings, everyone. You've all been so supportive of my new venture, and my goal is to help you be successful like me. So today I'm answering some of your questions."*

Viviane clicked her mouse, and the video paused. "She was at her house, in her backyard, making that video about her new business that just launched. It's got a time stamp from the upload that shows five twenty-two."

"That answers that question." Hoyt shrugged.

Rebecca shook her head. "You can upload videos from your phone too. Or preschedule posts. She could've been anywhere when that was posted. Is there a way to find out where it was uploaded from?"

"Is anyone back there?" Rhonda's voice rang out from the lobby.

Rolling her eyes at the intrusion, Rebecca sighed.

Viviane snickered, and Hoyt covered his mouth. Most likely to hide his grin.

The day had been going so well without Rhonda there asking all kinds of questions and breathing down her neck. "We're here, Rhonda. What's up? Why didn't you call ahead?" She walked to the front and buzzed the woman in.

Rhonda was dressed more casually than Rebecca had ever seen her. She was in a sleeveless button-up shirt, capris, and a pair of sandals. "Because I was hoping *not* to find you here on a Saturday." She frowned at Rebecca, then walked past her into the bullpen and addressed the deputies there, leaving Rebecca to trail behind her. "Does she ever take a day off?"

"Not that I've ever seen." Hoyt shook his head.

"You mean a whole day?" Viviane laughed. "Does going over case notes at home count?"

"No, it does not." Rhonda spun on Rebecca as she approached. "Girl, seriously. Downtime is important, both for your physical and mental health. And you have deputies on shift. Why are you working on this lovely Saturday?"

Feeling more than a little attacked, Rebecca struggled to voice the obvious answer. Wasn't solving a murder enough reason to be working on the weekend?

Rhonda turned to the board. "And don't act like you haven't been working. That's your handwriting up there. The marker isn't even dry." She gestured dramatically, walking over to tap where Rebecca had just been writing.

"Jessica Fletcher's got you there." Hoyt kept his grin despite Rebecca scowling at him.

"I prefer to think of myself as a Matlock type of person. You know, if I were old and a man." Rhonda pondered that for a moment. "And a lawyer."

"Who's Jessica Fletcher?" Viviane looked as confused as

Rebecca felt, but clearly for different reasons. "And who's Matlock? Are they with the state police?"

"Before your time, Vi. They were the television sleuths who inspired generations." Rhonda spun around yet again, flinging her pointing finger toward Rebecca. "And why haven't you asked me yet why I'm in town?"

Giving in to the insanity, Rebecca threw her arms up in defeat. "Rhonda, why are you in town?"

"I'm so glad you asked." Rhonda straightened and grinned with a bit of a sparkle in her eye. "I have a six-pack of that awful coffee stout you love so much, a bottle of good red for me, and three pounds of shrimp straight from the boat. We keep saying we need to get together for dinner one of these days, so I decided today is that day. Since it is, you know, your day off."

"You just randomly decided on today?" Rebecca didn't believe her.

Rhonda huffed. "That, and I have to be in town early in the morning to talk with Arthur Carson, the bank manager, so I thought it best to come down the night before and get a room. Then I saw a guy selling shrimp from his boat and thought I should get enough for us to have dinner together. Except I don't have a stove, oven, or anything really in my motel room. Can I use your kitchen, and I'll split my food with you and Ryker? I've been wanting to meet him anyway."

Rebecca looked at the board, at her deputies who were failing to hide their amusement, and at Rhonda who was so excited at the idea of shrimp that she was actually leaning forward, waiting for an answer.

Well, hell. Rebecca was hungry, but more than that, she was intensely curious as to why Rhonda was acting this way.

"Okay, fine. We'll go have shrimp."

Rhonda did a little victory dance.

"Frost, Darby, check into the Fairbanks and give me a holler if anything comes up."

Rhonda strode over and linked her arm through Rebecca's. "Better yet, don't call. We have alcohol that needs drinking! Come on, Rebecca, it's time you learned about the salt life."

34

They'd gotten to Rebecca's house and explained what was going on to Ryker, who'd been more than happy to have different company for the evening. And to eat something other than frozen casseroles for once. He'd been so happy, in fact, that he'd offered to cook the shrimp and told them to enjoy their drinks on the porch while he worked.

"He's cooked for me before, and it was pretty good. It was shrimp pasta that time too." Rebecca leaned back and kicked her feet out in front of her. Rhonda had been right about one thing, downtime was good.

What she didn't want to admit was how crowded her house had felt for the last week or so. Ryker wasn't a problem roommate. Not at all. But she wasn't used to living with someone else. Or that someone else having company over. The extra people were necessary to help him while she recovered, so she never complained. The feeling of being cramped never went away, though.

Now that she was thinking about it, that might have been why she was so testy with Rhonda the last few days. At least she'd had her office as a quiet place. Then, enter Rhonda.

The clank of pots and pans echoed out from the open back door, and she took a hefty pull of her beer. Humphrey was the only one that wasn't getting on her nerves recently, and he was inside at his master's feet, hoping Ryker would drop some shrimp heads for him.

"You didn't tell me he could cook too." Rhonda leaned over the patio table to whisper to Rebecca. "How about you? Do you cook?" Rhonda swirled her wine in the glass they'd managed to find in the cupboards. She insisted that the Beaujolais she'd chosen would pair well with the seafood.

"I can, when I have time." Rebecca tipped back her beer again. "I'm not bad at it either. I just have so little time."

Rhonda snorted into her glass. "Maybe if you didn't go in on your day off, you would."

Rebecca sighed. "I only went in to finish up some paperwork."

"You could've done that from your laptop. Don't try to fool me." Rhonda smirked at her, then stopped. She squinted at Rebecca and dropped her voice. "That's not the real reason you went in, was it?"

Rebecca looked over her shoulder at the open door where the sounds of cooking were getting louder. Without a word, Rhonda nodded her understanding.

"Big changes are hard to handle. And you've had a lot of them stacked on top of each other recently."

Truer words had never been spoken. "I don't regret it. But sometimes a woman just needs a bit of peace and quiet, you know? I've been…it's not easy."

Rebecca felt disloyal talking about Ryker like that. It wasn't his fault. He'd gotten hurt because he'd involved himself in a case she and Rhonda had been working on.

Rebecca knew what she was signing up for when she said he could stay with her.

"It's okay, you know, to feel however you need to feel."

Now Rhonda was a shrink? "I used to have every morning and evening to myself. After work, I could just sit here, in silence. Listen to music. Read a book."

"Dance like no one's watching." Rhonda added with a smile. "The weird little things we do when we're alone, but you'd never want your new boyfriend to see you doing. How long have you been together?"

"Together? That's a hard question to answer. We weren't even really dating, just trying to date with his busy schedule and mine. We never even made it official, really. But less than a month. Then we went a month without talking while he was in the hospital and I was recovering. I thought he'd broken up with me, but that was just his mom trying to keep him away from me."

"*Eash*! He let his parents steamroll you like that?" Rhonda grimaced so hard her neck tightened.

Rebecca instantly felt like she needed to defend Ryker. She wasn't the kind of person who sat around bashing her boyfriend when hanging out with her friends. "He was vulnerable. Who else was going to make medical decisions for him? He was in a coma. It wasn't like he had any say over anything. And they told him I hadn't called."

"Sounds like there's a lot of drama between you two already. And your relationship is so fresh."

"There's a lot of drama, period." Rebecca took another drink, shocked to find she'd finished her beer so quickly. "This is just one more piece of it. Besides, once he's better, he can go back to his house. I'm helping him out because I harbor guilt for how he got hurt and because his parents are apparently traveling. For right now, he just needs someone around to catch on if his memory starts going fuzzy again."

"And is it? He seems pretty put together to me." Rhonda gestured toward the house. "I'd hate to think I'm making him work hard if he's not up for it. I can go inside and whip up something with whatever you've got in those cupboards too. I'm no slouch when it comes to food."

Rebecca chuckled at that. Rhonda lived for food. She'd once told Rebecca that one of the reasons she became a state trooper was so that she could travel around the state, and no one would think twice about her eating out so much. In fact, most restaurants gave her a discount. "Some days are worse than others. But he's getting better."

"That's good to hear." Rhonda sipped her wine and stared out at the ocean. "I know I told you that downtime is good, but I have one more thing about work I wanted to fill you in on."

"Oh?" Rebecca braced herself. With how deep Rhonda had been diving into the old files, she assumed she'd come up with something sooner or later. "Let's hear it."

"You remember your case with the sleep-talking assassin and his pill popping girlfriend?"

Rebecca was about to get up to get another beer but stopped at the question. Caught off guard, she nodded. This wasn't one of Wallace's cases at all. It was hers and only ten days old. "Dwight Stokely and Sophia Maryland. Yeah, what about them?"

"I read the transcript and noticed the brief series of numbers he kept reciting after the names. I looked them up. They're the last few digits of account numbers for your local Sandpiper Bank. That's why I'm meeting with the bank manager tomorrow."

Rebecca frowned. "On a Sunday?"

"Yeah. We're trying to keep it under the radar since it's such a sensitive meeting. Hopefully he can give me some information on them. Like, if they match the names Stokely was rambling on about too. If so, we can try to match withdrawals to Stokely's deposits. We don't have enough evidence to go after the Yacht Club members directly, but maybe if we dig through the accounts that came up in another case, we can start putting together a bit more of the puzzle and find something to nail these guys on."

"And Arthur Carson is willing to give you that information? He insisted on having a warrant before."

Rhonda smiled and patted her pocket. "I know what a stickler he is for the red tape. I read your files, remember?"

Rebecca stood up, shaking her head. If they could get their hands on the bank accounts of the Yacht Club, it would be child's play to start connecting the different members to the criminals they already knew were associated with them. They could find the rest of them too. The ones Wallace hadn't found because he'd never had reason to try and arrest them. People like Richmond Vale and Mitchell Longfellow.

"That kind of good news deserves another beer." She turned for the door and paused, seeing Ryker standing there. "Hey, babe, what's up?"

"Humphrey." Ryker pushed the door open, and the chocolate lab ran out to jump on Rebecca. "He's not as much of a fan of shrimp as he thought he was. Are you coming in already? Dinner won't be ready for another ten minutes or so."

Rebecca waved her empty bottle, and he laughed.

"Oh, I see. Tonight's a serious drinking night." He headed for the fridge, and Rebecca peered around him.

There were two pans on the stove and a pot of water with pasta boiling in it.

"Mmm, it smells good in here." She tried to sneak closer to the stove to see what was cooking to go with the shrimp, but he shooed her off with a laugh.

"You're as bad as Humphrey." He opened the fridge door and handed her another beer, taking the empty one from her. "Go on, talk with your friend, relax. You deserve this."

Rebecca smiled and rose to give him a quick kiss on the lips. "Thanks, babe." Maybe living with someone wasn't so bad.

35

I should've done this weeks ago. After all, he deserved it. I crept through the side yard once again. This time, I was determined not to lose my nerve or be interrupted. Once I did this, everything could go back to normal. I could live the good life. The life he'd said I could have when he talked me into taking this dark path in the first place.

The heavy citrus scent of the citronella guided me through the predawn darkness. Thick clouds covered the sky. Maybe it would rain. We could use it to clean the air and wash away all the things that have happened on our island, all the filth that'd been piling up.

As I expected, he was finishing his early morning swim. I'd learned his schedule, and my timing was perfect. He dried off and threw his unappealing body onto a chaise lounge. As during my first visit, he sprawled out wearing nothing but his robe and his tiny swimsuit.

The water in the pool was calm following his feeble attempt at exercise. This was probably the only time he used it. What was the point of all his wealth? To have a pool he rarely swam in, a sterile fire that burned with the push of a button, and a house that no one else lived in? Was this what it was like to have power and wealth?

If so, maybe I didn't want it. Not this much, at least. Just enough money to make life a bit easier, to start a family of my own one day. I watched the fire dance and flicker. The light was calm and soothing. So was the gentle *shush* of the pool pump as it kicked on.

No, if I ever had a chance to live a life like this, I'd enjoy every bit of it. Early morning swims in the pool. Gatherings around a real fire with friends and marshmallows. A cobblestone patio without a single weed. That was the life.

He didn't deserve all the nice things. He'd gotten wealthy off people like me. Lending money at ridiculous interest rates, knowing we could never repay the loan—indebted to this piece of human garbage.

I deserved the life he had. Other than the guy on the boat, I'd never hurt anyone.

Taking a deep breath, I let it out and pushed the rest of the way through the dew-covered plants that formed the wall around his backyard, invading his space. He glanced up when he saw me, startled, then sought to regain his composure before going back to whatever he was reading on his tablet.

He was trying to play it cool, but I could see my presence was an unwelcome surprise. "How dare you trespass? I have half a mind to call the authorities."

"Oh, I don't think you'd do that. You wouldn't want me to tell them what you did."

"What *I* did? My dear, I was nowhere near those docks when you torched those boats. More importantly, I was with my alibi when you murdered a man."

Crap. He had an alibi. I could only hope my alibi was as sound.

Although he still seemed unnerved by my presence, he faked his bravado. "What are you doing here? Come to pay down some of your interest? Did you rethink my offer?"

My skin crawled as his eyes swept over my body.

"I'm not here to pay you. Or accept any more of your poisonous offers." I raised my arm and pointed my gun. "But I am here to give you what you deserve."

He paled. "Put that away before it goes off in your shaky hand." He might have been mocking my unsteadiness as I grasped the grip of the gun, but his own hand shook as he tried to act casual and swipe the page of whatever he was browsing on his tablet. "You all come asking for money or a favor. I have faith in your dreams enough to try and help you succeed. When you inevitably fail and it's time to pay the piper, you blame me."

"Because it's all your fault." Anger rattled my right hand, and I had to grip it with my left, too, just to keep the gun steady.

"For what?" He finally set his tablet down on the paver stones beneath his chair and stared at me. "For giving you money? For giving you opportunity? Am I to blame for you not being able to do either of your jobs properly? All you had to do was what you promised me you could do. Make money so you could pay me back. I don't run a charity. Maybe you shouldn't have tried to launch a business. Men are better suited for such pursuits. And because you failed, you've ended up in a predicament."

The gun was growing heavier by the second. "I was a fool to trust you."

"I agree you were a fool, but not for trusting me. I'm honestly surprised you managed to burn my boat." He rolled his eyes. "But you did screw up. No one was supposed to be killed."

Tears burned my eyes, and I blinked them away. "When Mac came aboard, I had no choice. I had to stop him from calling the police. Then the fire got really bad. But I still threw the canister of oil and made sure to light it so the fire would spread to your stupid boat. And because of me, it went up in flames like you wanted." Both hands were shaking now, and I couldn't seem to stop them.

"What you call quick on your feet, I believe dear Sheriff West calls arson and murder. You're a stupid woman who thinks she can run with the big boys. Well, you can't. You don't have it in you. That's something you've proved time and again." He waved at the weapon, looking no more afraid than if I were holding a paper clip.

"I—"

"Put your gun down. Maybe if you come over here and get down on your knees, I can find a reason not to call the cops on you. You can't repay me if you're in jail." He pushed his robe aside and spread his legs wider.

"I'm not stupid." I took a step closer, and he smiled. That vicious, reptilian smile. "Maybe I can't run with the big boys, like you say."

I took another step.

"That's right. You can't." He smiled as if he'd won some game between us. But he didn't know I wasn't playing anymore.

"Which means..." I picked up the pillow from the other chair and held it in front of my gun to muffle the sound.

With that movement, he finally seemed to catch on. His arms and legs began to thrash, as if he were attempting to retreat into his chaise lounge.

"I need to remove some people from the race in order to advance."

Staring into his shocked eyes, I pulled the trigger. His

body jerked, and tufts of cotton floated through the air. Blood poured out of his chest, trickling down his belly and soaking into his robe.

Before long, another larger stream started gurgling out from his back. It would stain the expensive cobblestone in no time.

The propane fire pit would do nothing to comfort him as his blood ran free. The designer pillow had barely muffled the sound of the shot. I could only hope the noise from the pool pump had covered some of it. Either way, I knew I couldn't stick around.

His jaw fell open, his chin slumping onto his chest.

I'd done it. I'd really done it.

Relief raced through me as a laugh escaped. Pressing my fingers to my lips, I turned and hurried away, leaving him and all the horror he'd brought to my life behind me. Hidden behind a fake wall, next to a faux fire, where no one would look because no one cared about him.

Finally, a new day was dawning, and my life would be the way it should've been all along.

36

"Why is it that the more money you have, the worse your taste gets?" Hoyt grabbed the camera from the glove box and looked up and down the street fronting Chapman's McMansion. "My boys made houses out of toy blocks just like this when they were kids, except theirs were colorful, at least. All blues, reds, yellows, and greens."

All these houses lacked style and personality. Each featured a huge front window, though there was nothing worth looking at on the street. Even the brightening sky, turning a hazy pink, couldn't make the houses sparkle.

At Hoyt's side, Viviane scanned the street as well. "Why do I have the feeling you're talking about Zach and Adam building li'l houses?"

"Because that's exactly what I'm talking about." Hoyt motioned at the house in front of them. "Grab the tape and start setting up the crime scene perimeter while I check the house."

While their boss headed to the hospital to try and get a statement from the victim, the rest of them had been sent to his home to scour it for evidence and secure the scene.

Whoever attacked Chapman had shot him outside, by the pool, but that didn't stop Hoyt from checking the house as he approached the front entrance and tried the doorknob. It was locked.

He pounded his fist on it, unsure if anyone was inside. Nobody else was listed as a resident, but that didn't necessarily mean anything. One of the cleaning crew had called the police after finding Chapman bleeding out poolside. Except for that one piece of action this morning, the neighborhood seemed dead otherwise.

Once they cleared the scene and got backup there, they'd need to ask the neighbors if they saw or heard anything.

The door opened, and a woman in a polo shirt and tan pants stood there. Her blond hair was pulled back in a severe bun, which made her pale skin seem tight and thin on her face. "Can I help you?"

Hoyt tapped his badge on his chest. "Deputy Frost. Are you aware the owner of this property was shot?"

"I know, I'm with the cleaning service. My name is Savannah Bleu."

"Were you the one to call nine-one-one?"

"Yes, sir."

"We need to secure the premises." He gestured broadly, encompassing the lawns behind him as well as the house. "This entire property is a crime scene."

She nodded, her jaw tight and her voice tense. "I understand."

"You haven't cleaned anything up, have you? Touched anything?"

She shook her head. "His regular housekeeper is elsewhere. I was just holding down the fort until the police arrived. Mr. Chapman requires that his house be cleaned while he's out back by the pool. He pays well, so we accommodate his request. The house is all yours." With that, she stepped out the door and started to walk away.

"Ma'am, we're going to need to get a statement from you. But first, we have to clear the residence. I need you to wait on the front lawn. Then Deputy Darby can take your statement. Viviane!" Hoyt called for his trainee.

Hearing her name, Viviane tied off the crime scene tape and headed over.

"Deputy Darby, we need to secure the house. Then go ahead and take Ms. Bleu's statement for me."

Viviane jerked her head up and gazed at the woman. "Thank you for your patience, ma'am. I'll be with you as soon as we're done."

Hoyt and Viviane made quick work of clearing the home. He'd been impressed that she hadn't made any mistakes. The process had been quick with none of Viviane's actions requiring correction or instruction.

He stepped onto the front porch once the home was secured while Viviane talked to Savannah Bleu on the sidewalk. Hoyt checked the doorbell. It was a basic one, no cameras involved. A quick search along the eaves showed no cameras hiding there either.

Walking along the front of the house, he reached the corner and turned to the backyard. Long, thin bushes of citronella swayed in the wind, forming a privacy wall. Checking around his feet, he walked the perimeter of the house, looking for any evidence.

According to the report he got from the Coastal Ridge Police Department, the housekeeper found Chapman by the pool after not being able to get in through the front door. Which likely meant the shooter walked through the side yard.

The head-height stand of citronella closest to the house was smashed and bent, as if something had trudged through it, going in both directions. Hoyt took several pictures as he walked closer. Stopping, he took a picture straight down, where the plant had been trampled and several new shoots had been flattened, grinding the delicate fibers into pulp.

With his long legs, it was easy enough to move through the fragrant plant and reach the other side. He took several more pictures of the flattened foliage before turning to consider the patio.

There was no doubt this was where the shooting had occurred. A rattan chaise lounge chair was saturated in blood, and pools of dark crimson had soaked into the stone pavers below—though one paver looked odd, all buff and shiny. Flying insects of all types had swarmed to the area, feasting on the iron-rich meal.

Snapping pictures so fast it would make a tourist jealous, Hoyt moved forward. He had to adjust angles a few times because the morning shadows wreaked havoc with the photo composition. He was only about four feet from the chair when he saw a glint in the grass and knelt down.

Sitting on top of the perfectly maintained patch beside the patio was a single shell casing. It looked to be a 9mm. He took several pictures before getting on his radio to ask Viviane to bring evidence markers back to him.

Chapman appeared to have been sitting in this chair, holding his tablet when he was shot. He either dropped it or set it down. His seated position most likely had created a waterfall of blood from his lap that poured rapidly before winding down to a trickle as his heart beat slower and slower.

Walking carefully to avoid disturbing any evidence, Hoyt approached the back door. It was standing wide open with cold air blowing out as the air-conditioning tried to keep up with the rising temperatures outside.

"Frost, you back here?" Jake's voice snapped Hoyt out of his thoughts.

"Yep. You should be able to step through the break in the bushes. Just make sure you don't step on anything." Hoyt took several pictures of the back door before joining the newest deputy.

Breaking through the plants as easily as Hoyt had, Jake held up an evidence kit. "Darby asked me to bring this to you. Where do you want me to start?"

"With the trampled plants. It looks like the shooter came in and out the same way." Hoyt pointed out the shell he'd found. "And we've got a shell casing right here."

Jake nodded and set the kit down. "Where are you going to be?"

Hoyt grinned. "Inside. There's no way I'm letting an opportunity like this pass me by. I'm going to record everything I'm legally allowed to in his home office before his lawyers get here and bog down the process. Since, you know, I'd be derelict in my duties if I didn't check everything."

37

When Rebecca's phone chirped, she read the status updates from Viviane and Hoyt. Another message pinged in from the Coastal Ridge Police Department, confirming Oswald Chapman was undergoing treatment for a gunshot wound.

Chapman was still alive.

In the middle of all those messages, the fax machine started grinding.

"Guess everyone has something to say today." There had to be better ways to start a Sunday morning than juggling a million different tasks.

"Hello, Sheriff." Rhonda stood on the other side of the half door, holding up a box of croissants.

"Come on in." Rebecca buzzed Rhonda into the bullpen, then headed to the fax machine. "DNA results are in." She held up the document she'd just received. "We've got a match for our John Doe."

"Is it MacDaniel?" Rhonda passed over the box from Bean Tree and took the paper. "Have you made the notification yet, or do you want me to go with you?"

Rebecca smelled the raspberry steam seeping from the croissant bag and opened it. "Yes, it's MacDaniel. If you're coming with me, we'll have to do a couple unpleasant errands together. I need to go check on Oswald Chapman. He was shot early this morning."

She hoisted out a croissant and took a big bite. Her eyes rolled into the back of her head in ecstasy.

Rhonda frowned at her.

"Sorry, did you not intend to share?" She wiped the buttery crumbs from the corners of her lips.

"Oh, no. I brought those to share. Food tastes better with company."

"Thanks." Realizing the special agent had more to say, Rebecca held up her hand. "I really need to get over to the hospital to see if I can get a statement from Chapman. You're welcome to join me."

Rhonda nodded, and the two women took the box of croissants as they headed to Rebecca's SUV. Once they were settled in the vehicle and headed to Coastal Ridge, Rhonda broke the silence. "This isn't the purpose of my visit, but I'd be remiss if I didn't point this out. I'm worried that you seem to favor Deputy Darby. Not a lot, mind you. But as a professional, I wanted to make sure you were aware of your slight bias, especially since Frost seems to have the same one."

Rebecca bristled and immediately realized that was proof of her bias as her first instinct was to defend Viviane by downplaying her own actions. "I know. I'm doing my best. Viviane and I were friends before she became a deputy, and she was my dispatcher too. It's been a struggle, reminding myself not to be too lenient or too hard on her."

Rhonda nodded sympathetically and snagged one of the croissants. "I can imagine. It's not something I've had to deal with myself, but it's got to be rough, switching from a friend and dispatcher who you're meant to protect to a deputy standing beside you." She swallowed hurriedly. "I've been struggling with that this entire week too. Professional and personal boundaries."

"Is that why you keep trying to insert yourself into my investigation even though you're supposed to be working on something else entirely?" Rebecca snapped before she could stop herself, but Rhonda laughed it off.

"No, that's because I'm a nosy person who can't see a puzzle without wanting to solve it. I did try to at least be helpful, like setting up the murder board to get started." She sighed dramatically, pressing the back of her wrist to her forehead. "Before I went to my closet to read through hundreds of piles of dusty old papers."

Rebecca snorted as she took the turn onto the bridge. "That 'closet' you're talking about is my office."

"Uh, no. Actually, it was the records closet in Coastal Ridge. It's not like I started my investigation down here, taking over your office. That was only the bits where I needed your input. Everything is filling up my office in Norfolk." She gestured around the cruiser. "I'm glad no one can overhear this. I think you were right about that conspiracy theory of yours."

Excitement thrilled up Rebecca's nerves, and she chanced a quick glance over to the passenger seat. "Seriously? Did you find something?"

"Lots of somethings. And *someones*. This is bigger than even you thought."

"So are you going to tell me about it?"

"Nope." Rhonda stared at the side of Rebecca's face. "Not because I don't trust you or think you'll act too early or anything, but because I'm having my findings double- and triple- checked. And only by people I know I can trust.

Which is going to take time. And to ensure everyone's safety, I'm not going to spill any names."

Rebecca squeezed the steering wheel. "No names at all?"

Rhonda grimaced. "I will say that, as far as I know, you can trust all your deputies and your dispatchers. But we're still digging."

"We?" Rebecca pushed the issue. Who was Rhonda working with? "Weren't you supposed to meet with Arthur Carson today? How did that go?"

"So now that we have confirmation of the victim's identity, what's our next course of action?" Rhonda's face gave nothing away.

Realizing Rhonda wasn't going to answer her questions, Rebecca was left with two choices—either ignore Rhonda and go dig around to find the answers herself or trust Rhonda to do her job properly and move forward with her own work. Knowing she could just ask the bank manager later about the meeting, she decided to leave it alone.

"We look into motives for killing Mac while also expanding our possible suspect list to include others on the outer edges of this investigation. With Chapman's shooting, we need to find someone with a motive to harm either or both of the men...to see if the crimes are even connected. We don't yet know if MacDaniel was a target, but we'll chase down every piece of evidence until we get the answers we need."

Rebecca parked the cruiser in the parking garage shared by the hospital and the forensic department. The same garage where she and Hoyt had been jumped by a bunch of Aqua Mafia goons sent to scare Rebecca off her then-fledgling investigation into the Yacht Club. "The fire marshal is certain the origin of the fire was on the *Shoreline Catch*. We'll focus on that and on MacDaniel and Chapman, then move outward from there."

"What about the girl who ran from you? Serenity." Rhonda unbuckled her seat belt and turned toward Rebecca. "Did her alibi ever get solidified?"

"That's a hard one. If she had a vehicle, she could've just barely gotten from dinner with her parents in a public place to the boat to set it on fire. That'd be all she'd have had time for. But she claims she was on foot."

"Yeah, but her story about going jogging after dinner is pretty flimsy. Who goes for a long jog directly after eating dinner?" Rhonda stuck her tongue out in disgust. "A pleasant walk, I could understand. But a jog? All that bouncing and shifting with a full stomach? And who wears clothes to jog in to their birthday dinner at a restaurant?"

"She claims she used that as an excuse not to ride with her parents after they'd been drinking." Rebecca eyed the croissant resting on a napkin on the console and took another bite.

"Which goes to prove she's an excellent liar and won't hesitate to do so, even if it's not about something important, like staying out of jail. You need to clear that up. It's just too convenient that she found herself at the dock right as the fire happened. No matter what she says about seeing smoke."

"I saw the smoke from my house, Rhonda. And she was much closer to it than I was. A lot of people did, and we all came running, the same as her." Rebecca chewed slowly, as if she were thinking things through. "If she's a suspect, then so is everyone else who showed up to help put the fire out. Myself included."

Though Rhonda didn't relent, she also didn't argue further.

Rebecca typed out a message to Hoyt, asking him to expand the search to include the families of the Fairbanks and Ballards. She also asked him to thoroughly process Chapman's house, even though she doubted he'd need any prompting to do that.

Finally, if she didn't finish at the hospital before they were done at the newest crime scene, she asked him to stop by Selena's Eatery to see if they had CCTV that showed the McCreedys eating and what time they left.

Rhonda threw open the passenger door and waited for Rebecca. "I wonder if anyone knows where Serenity is right now."

38

"Sheriff West and Special Agent Lettinger." Rebecca held her badge up as she approached the nurses' station. "We got a call about a gunshot victim, Oswald Chapman."

The nurse, a middle-aged man with wide swaths of gray in his chin stubble, looked up. "Sheriff West, yes. Sorry it took so long to get in touch with you. We called the police when we realized what we had, but," he ran a hand over tired eyes, "it got complicated. Let me get the doctor on duty to come talk to you."

"We'd be fine just talking with the victim." Rhonda put her badge away, her gaze scanning the ICU wing around them.

"That won't be possible. He's not awake." The nurse already had the phone to his ear and punched in a combination of buttons. "In fact, he's just out of surgery as of thirty minutes ago. The doctor can explain it all to you."

He hung up the phone, then politely and professionally ignored them.

They were left waiting, standing in the hallway, as staff

and family members passed through the corridors. Rebecca kept an eye out for anybody she recognized but saw no one. She tried to think of what could've led to this.

Was it at all connected to the dock fire?

Was this just another seemingly random act of violence brought about by Yacht Club scheming? Or had the island's curse sparked into Shadow's flame?

Or maybe the fire was supposed to take him and his boat out at the same time, and someone was cleaning up loose ends. They had to get to the bottom of who started the fire and why.

An older man in a long physician's coat walked up to the desk, and Rebecca straightened from where she'd been leaning against the wall. He spoke to the nurse, then turned to face her.

"Sheriff West?"

She pulled her badge out and nodded, Rhonda doing the same. He waved her and Rhonda over. "I'm Doctor Terrell, the attending physician in the ER. To break it down, just after five thirty this morning, we received a patient via ambulance. The man presented with a gunshot wound to the chest and extreme blood loss. Unfortunately, his already tenuous condition was exacerbated by hypothermia, increasing his blood loss."

The doctor checked his watch. "I've managed to keep him alive for the last four hours but barely. He's out of surgery and recovering, but he's not out of the woods yet. He'll need careful monitoring, and we don't expect him to wake up anytime soon. The gunshot went through his chest without hitting anything vital. I managed to retain some fragments, and I'll send those along."

"Thank you. Was he awake at all? Did he say who did

this?" Rebecca knew it was a wild hope, but there was always a chance.

"Actually, he came around when we were carrying him back. He kept saying, 'I can't believe she shot me.'"

"She?" That was a surprise. "You're sure that's what he said?"

"Oh, yes. He also said something about a contract on his desk. I don't know what that's about." He gestured to a hall on their left. "If you'll excuse me, I have other patients."

Rhonda waited until the doctor was out of earshot, then mumbled. "Serenity is a she."

Rebecca nodded her agreement. "So is Kym McCreedy. And Addison Fairbank. For that matter, so is the housekeeper who called this in. As are you and I."

"And about half the population, sure. But the only one who made the first round of suspects is Serenity. We need to double-check her alibi."

"We will. Selena's doesn't open this early in the offseason. So far, we have Serenity's statement, the corroboration of her parents, a time-stamped call to her mom about the fire, and a cash app transfer to her father to cover her dinner." Rebecca waved her hand for Rhonda to follow her out of the hospital.

"I'd like to speak with her myself." Rhonda pulled her phone from her pocket as they walked and started typing out a message, dodging walls and bystanders with practiced ease. "Just let me notify my office that Chapman is down, so they can run a check to see if any other movers and shakers know about this yet."

That sounded incredibly interesting to Rebecca, but she kept her mind on the case they were working on instead.

She typed out her own quick message to Hoyt. *Check for a contract on Chapman's desk.*

Already done, Hoyt replied. He also sent an attachment, but she'd have to wait to open it for the moment.

"What makes you think he meant Serenity when he said, 'she shot me?'" Rebecca asked. "You immediately jumped to that conclusion."

Rhonda tucked her own phone away, lifted her head, and checked their surroundings. Apparently, she was satisfied no one could hear her. "Let's just say I know a bit more about what Serenity has been up to than you do. I'll fill you in later."

39

"By all means, take the lead here." Rebecca waved Rhonda ahead to approach the door of the McCreedy household. "Since you seem to know more about Serenity and what she's doing, I'll just hang back."

Rhonda shot her an exasperated look. "Really?"

Rebecca shook her head. "I'm not being sarcastic. I'm serious. That, and Serenity is terrified of me, or so she says."

That froze Rhonda in her tracks. "Why would she be terrified of you but not me? No offense, Rebecca, but I do have more legal authority here than you do."

Is she...jealous that she's not the scary one?

"Because most of what she remembers from her attack is me yelling. And she's never gone to therapy for the PTSD, even though I encouraged her to go. And...I'm the sheriff. You ask the questions."

Rebecca waited a full step behind Rhonda, not willing to budge on this. She trusted that the special agent had more insight into Serenity's recent history, but she still didn't believe the young woman had anything to do with the fires,

Bolivar MacDaniel's murder, or the attempted murder of Oswald Chapman.

The stalemate between them was broken when the house's front door opened, though neither woman had yet made it up the walkway. Eustace McCreedy strode out, a suitcase in each hand, followed by his wife, who was carrying two of her own.

"Sheriff West?" Eustace peered at her over his aviator glasses. "Did you need something else?"

Rhonda stepped forward, pulling her badge and flashing it. "Actually, I do. I'm Special Agent Lettinger with the state police. I'd like to speak to your daughter, Serenity McCreedy."

Eustace frowned and looked back at his wife before answering. "But she's not here. She left yesterday."

Rebecca could almost hear Rhonda's teeth grind. "What time yesterday and where did she go?"

"Back to New York. She's got to get ready for her new job. We told your people about it, Sheriff. Serenity has a job now and can't be held back by small-town drama like this anymore."

Kym waved their concerns away with casual disregard. "She's an adult now, doing adult things, and has her own apartment."

Rhonda took a threatening step forward, and Kym pulled back, ducking into the doorway of the house. "When did she leave?"

"I don't know. Sometime yesterday after talking with the sheriff. We were out and when we came back, her room was all packed up. She took all her clothes and her car and left. I assume it was for her work." Serenity's stepmother gave a tiny laugh and tossed her hair. "It's not like she left us a note with time stamps listing her intentions. She's a grown woman and can do as she pleases. I expect she'll call her father or me once she's settled in. We'll let you know then."

Rebecca couldn't help but respond to Kym's blasé answer. "Even after what happened to her best friend just three months ago, you didn't bother to make sure she arrived safely? That she's okay?"

Rhonda stormed up the path. "I'm going to need to search the house to make sure she's not hiding here somewhere."

Kym gave an indignant squeak but didn't protest as Rhonda pushed past her and into the house. "Her room's on the right. Toward the back. Let me show you."

Eustace stood there, watching everything transpire, and didn't say a word.

Rebecca turned her attention to him, Serenity's only remaining biological parent. He at least looked a bit concerned. "Do you even care that your daughter could be in danger? Or that she might have killed a man in an act of revenge?"

"No." He shook his head, then ashamedly bit his lip. "I didn't, I mean, I *do* care about my daughter, Sheriff. And I don't appreciate you implying otherwise. But I cannot believe that she was involved in any murder, the fire, any of it."

At this, Rhonda stopped just inside the doorway and turned. "She was nearly murdered herself. Don't you think that affected her? Changed her in some way?"

Before he could answer, Rebecca stepped in, keeping her voice low in case Serenity was in earshot. "I gave you the victims' rights pamphlets, yet it doesn't seem she ever used them. She never got therapy. She was a minor, and you didn't get her the help she needed. Instead, you let her go back to the man who's been using her for at least a year. The man who you *have to know* is involved with people committing child sex trafficking."

Eustace stared at her, his jaw hanging open slightly. He flinched as Rhonda, done with inspecting the interior, stormed back out of the house and toward the cruiser. "I've got her vehicle information. I'm sending out a BOLO. Anyone who runs like this has a damn good reason for it. I'm going to find Serenity McCreedy."

Rebecca stared at Eustace but directed her words to Rhonda. "Serenity isn't who you think she is. She's just a girl who lost her mother, lost her best friend, saw the devastation that can happen when fathers fail their kids, and fell in with some powerful people who promised her a better life. And then they used her for their own gain. She's not a cold-blooded killer, she's an abused and manipulated kid who needs someone to finally give a damn."

Serenity's father remained mute, watching the two women talk about his child.

"Maybe if we catch her in time, we can stop her from doing anything else that screws up her life."

Rebecca couldn't argue that, so she turned and walked to the cruiser. As she did, she pulled up the attachment Hoyt had sent earlier. Opening it with one hand, she slid behind the steering wheel.

And then she grinned.

"What is it? Did the BOLO get a hit already?" Rhonda slammed the door behind her and belted in.

Rebecca set her phone on the console. "Frost found some new, very interesting evidence." Turning the wheel over, she executed a tight U-turn. "We're going to go have a talk with the Fairbanks."

40

"Why would Addison Fairbank want to take a loan from Oswald Chapman anyway? I thought her husband was doing well for himself."

Rebecca listened as Rhonda tried to wrap her head around the information Hoyt had obtained at Chapman's residence. She knew just how Rhonda felt. Everything was messier when dealing with the Aqua Mafia, but having the case come back to point at such a basic, blue-collar family was completely unexpected. "She's just launched her own career and probably needed start-up money." She eased the SUV into the residential neighborhood.

"Is that Addison Fairbank?" Rhonda pointed as Rebecca parked on the side of the street. There was a mid-twenties woman standing in the front yard, holding her phone out and clearly taking either pictures or a video of the front garden.

"No." Rebecca threw the SUV into park. "Addison is taller and has dyed balayage hair, not chestnut brown. I don't know who that is."

They got out of the SUV, catching the attention of the woman standing in front of the house.

She turned and gave them a timid smile. "Can I help you, Officer?" Her eyes tracked to Rhonda, making out the writing on her shirt. "Officers?"

In sync, they pulled their badges and identified themselves.

"Oh, Sheriff West. I've read about you. You're the one who busted those kidnappers from Lynnhaven, right? I'm from Coastal Ridge. I heard all about it." The brunette woman smiled as if she'd just met a celebrity.

Rebecca was immediately uncomfortable and at the same time felt vindicated, hearing it referred to as a Lynnhaven problem she'd solved, which wasn't inaccurate, since that was where the kidnappers had started before moving to her town. "And you are?"

"Oh, sorry. My name's Quincy Sandoval. I'm Addison Fairbank's intern." She twisted around and gestured to the house behind her.

Rhonda pointed at the empty driveway. "That's who we're here to see. Are the Fairbanks in?"

Quincy shook her head. "Not now. Addison was. She's the one who let me in. We were doing some edits. But then she had to run errands in town, and I decided to get some B-roll for her videos. She calls it 'showing initiative.' Isn't she so smart? A lot of her branding is to show how life can be easier when you work from home, so she has me take a lot of shots around the house."

"Is Cole around, then?" Rebecca glanced at the windows, checking to see if there was any movement in the house. With the carefree way Quincy was chatting, she worried she was trying to cover for the Fairbanks so they could get away.

"No, I'm pretty sure he's down at Shoreline Excursions."

Rebecca frowned. "His boat? That's in the evidence garage."

"Not the boat. His office down near the docks. The boat is named after his business, so they could use the branding for both things. That was one of Addison's ideas. She's so good at this. You know, she's the real reason Cole's business is flourishing, all the changes she's made. He's good at what he does, the fishing and stuff, but she's the real brains behind the operation. And I'm not just saying that because she's my mentor." Quincy beamed proudly.

"Online marketing and consulting. I remember reading that in the reports." Rebecca surveyed the yard and tried to peer inside the windows. From her vantage point, she couldn't see any movement inside the home.

"Yeah, she's a real rags to riches type of story. But Cole gets all the credit because he's the face of the business. He was barely keeping his business afloat before he married her, and she convinced him to let her take over the bills and everything. To him, she's just an employee and that's how he treats her. Of course, when other people are around, he acts like he'd be nowhere without her."

While she was talking, Quincy continued snapping photos of things Rebecca couldn't fathom would be useful to online marketing.

"Is a start-up like this expensive?"

Quincy's eyes went wide. "Yes. That's why I was so glad she was finally able to get that small business loan. With everything in her husband's name, she didn't have the credit to get a loan from a bank and it took a lot of digging to find someone who believed in her as much as I do. Now she can prove to the world that she's got what it takes, instead of always being in Cole's shadow."

"But now you're working for her, so you see everything

she's doing?" Rebecca glanced at the woman's phone screen to see if she was missing something in the photos.

"Not everything." Quincy moved to a different garden bed and began snapping more photos of a very plain-looking bush, at least in Rebecca's mind. "I mean, I only come here, like, one or two days a week. Addison does most of it on her own. But on days when Cole isn't here, I come down so I can act as her camera operator or whatever she needs. I'm learning so much from her, so I don't mind not getting paid."

"When was the last time you were here?" None of Quincy's actions were suspicious.

"Um." Quincy bit her lip. "Thursday, I think. Cole was visiting his mom, so we had the whole house to ourselves."

Rhonda had made her way over to the edge of the yard. "And you took video then? What did you record?"

"Oh, that day. Nothing. Addison had already shot and edited her video. But it was a timed piece, so she had me stay here with her phone so I could upload it using their Wi-Fi while she ran out to deal with some issue with the boat."

That got the attention of both Rhonda and Rebecca. "The boat?" Rebecca asked. "Which one?"

"I'm not sure. But when she came back, she reeked. I asked her about it, and she said the big tank had sprung a leak, and they'd need to get it repaired. That's why it's been out of commission this weekend. Which was fine. She'd already scheduled the next few fishing runs to go on the smaller boat. They couldn't take as many people out on those because the boat's on the small side. So Addison's plan was to simply schedule more tours. See? Smart."

Quincy kept working, not noticing Rebecca and Rhonda exchanging looks. Apparently, she didn't follow the news, or she'd have known about the fire.

"One more question, then we'll leave you alone. Do you know where Addison was going to run her errands?" Rebecca smiled at the younger woman while trying to keep her excitement under control. At this point, it wouldn't surprise her if Quincy offered to chauffeur them to Addison's last known location.

"Oh, yeah. She had to go do some paperwork down at Cole's office. Said it would take her a couple of hours."

"The same office where he is right now?"

Quincy gave a distracted "mm-hmm" and went on snapping.

Rebecca turned to Rhonda, who was already heading for the cruiser. "Thanks for your help, Quincy. We'll just head down there now, then."

"Yeah, sure. Always glad to help the police!" Quincy waved without lifting her gaze from her phone.

As they jogged to the SUV, Rhonda pulled her phone from her pocket. "Remind me again what Oswald Chapman's legal job is."

"He's an entrepreneur who specializes in payday loans. Loans with incredibly high interest rates. That's the interesting evidence I mentioned. Frost found a copy of the contract he had with Addison Fairbank in Oswald's office. I knew he was her backer even before Quincy spilled the beans." Rebecca yanked her door open and slid behind the wheel, turning the key in the ignition at the same time.

Rhonda was rounding the front of the cruiser when her phone rang, and she lifted it to her ear. Whatever the call was about was enough to slow her down and make her eyebrows jump several times.

Rebecca waved at her to hurry. They needed to get to Shoreline Excursions. If both Cole and Addison were there, they could be planning to run. That was, if Cole knew about what Addison had done.

Rhonda picked up the pace and launched herself into the vehicle, motioning for Rebecca to drive. "I got it. Thanks for letting me know." Dropping her phone, she pulled on her seat belt. "You are not going to believe who that was."

"After that one-woman show we just witnessed starring Quincy the fink, yes, I will."

"That was the FBI. They heard about Chapman being shot and wanted some information about it."

Hitting the gas, Rebecca headed for the docks. They were only a few minutes away. "What's he done to get their attention?"

"A lot, as it turns out. They were about to subpoena one of his boats for evidence in several felonies involving at least three other Yacht Club members." Rhonda pursed her lips.

"Let me guess. That boat would be the *Liquid Asset*." Rebecca took the next turn without slowing down. "He didn't need to worry about his insurance covering it because burning the boat was his 'insurance'...to ensure he didn't go to jail."

"But if Addison paid him back by burning his boat, why did she shoot him? Or was Cole the one who shot Chapman?"

Rebecca didn't have the answers. But one or both of the Fairbanks could be a killer.

41

The last of the documents were shredded. Every piece of paper that connected me to Oswald Chapman, the loan applications, banking details I'd had to assemble, the business plan I'd set up and failed to stick to for my launch. Every scrap of evidence from my long descent into desperation and madness that led to me working with that man was gone.

Oh god, what about any records *he* might have? I hadn't thought of that in my haste to off the creep. Now I'd have to go to his office and find a way to get into his files. No surprise that a woman's work was never done.

I picked up the bin of shreds and carried it into the back alley. There was a metal garbage can back there. I'd already emptied it, preparing for today. I upended the bin into the fire-safe canister. My shame, bad decisions, and mistakes. They'd soon go up in smoke. His files would be next.

Then I could finally start to build my success. Everything was in place. All the obstacles had been taken care of.

Reaching into my pocket, I pulled out the lighter I'd bought last week. Even that receipt had been shredded and added to the bin. "This is a goodbye to my wicked past. And a hello to my successful future." With that, I lit the paper on fire. It burned quickly, the tiny white pieces fluttering around in the can like foil in a snow globe.

"What the hell are you doing?"

I jumped at my husband's voice. He was in his office, staring out the back door at me like I'd grown a second head. "Getting rid of some old financial papers."

"Jeez, Addy, that's why we have a shredder. You don't think one fire was enough this week?" He stomped toward me, huffing angrily.

"Oh, it's just a tiny paper fire. Don't overreact." Sweat poured down my spine, and it was a struggle to keep my voice even. Still, his words got to me. "Besides, the business didn't even take a hit. We'll be better off next month than we were this month. Just you wait and see. And my business is about to go live too. So we'll be making at least twice as much."

He snorted, and my hackles jumped. After everything I had done, that was his reaction? Was he really so blind? So infatuated with his beloved lost boat that he still couldn't see me?

"That's good, honey. Because it's going to take a while to find a boat like the *Shoreline Catch*. I just heard back from the adjuster." He dropped the metal lid on the garbage can before it could finish burning. "That's why I came down here."

I wanted to jerk it away, to make sure all the bits had turned to ash, but I didn't. I stayed calm, smiling, happy for my husband. That was what a good wife did.

"She's basically irreplaceable. I don't know what I'm going to do without her. She was what made my business finally bloom, you know?"

No matter how good of a wife I was, he *still* loved that damn boat more than me. He gave all the credit and love to her!

I clenched my hands, fingertips striking the gun hidden in my pocket. Once I was done here, I'd planned to dump it in the ocean.

"You know what we haven't done in forever?" Just like I'd been taught by my mother, I made sure my smile reached my eyes. It had to if I was going to conceal the rage and jealousy burning inside me. "Taken a cruise by ourselves. Remember when we used to do that? Let's do that again."

He smiled back, that sweet, soft smile I remembered. "That's a great idea." Cole kissed me, and I just knew everything was going to work out. Soon I'd be making money of my own. Then he'd have proof of just how resourceful and smart I was. And I'd done it all myself. Without taking anything from him. Well, not anything that I hadn't helped him obtain in the first place.

"Let's do that as soon as I get the *Shoreline Catch II*."

This time when he smiled, my heart withered. "Isn't it bad luck to name a boat after one that sank?"

"Nah." He took my hand, and we walked inside the office. The tiny wisps of smoke had already dissipated from the back alley as he closed the door behind me. "You're thinking of when someone wants to rename a boat. That's where the bad luck comes in. Do you know where I left those sales pamphlets? Hey, in fact, we could ask to take some boats out for a test drive! That would be fun."

Cole started digging through his desk drawers, and my smile left my eyes. The anger came to the front and overtook me, just for a moment. There was a *thud* outside, and I spun away from him so he wouldn't see my real emotions.

"Who could be here on a Sunday? Your next reservation

isn't scheduled until tomorrow." I casually strolled to the windows.

My stomach dropped as I saw Sheriff West walking from her cruiser, heading straight for us. She looked up, and in that moment, facing her through the expansive windows, I knew she knew. Her eyes widened and filled with apprehension and a tinge of anger as soon as she saw me.

The poor sheriff must not have had a mother who taught her how to lie with her eyes.

I pulled the gun from my pocket. Maybe I wasn't done removing obstacles after all.

42

"She's got a gun!" Rebecca reached for her holster as she called out the warning to Rhonda.

Addison disappeared from the window, moving away from the door, farther into the office.

Dipping low, Rebecca sprinted for the wall next to the window where she'd have the most protection. Once she was safely tucked down, she spun around to check on Rhonda.

The special agent was peeking around the rear of the cruiser, safely out of sight.

Rebecca gestured to the side of the building and mouthed, *Back door.*

Rhonda nodded and took off at a sprint toward the alley.

"All units, I'm at the Bayview business strip. Suspect Addison Fairbank is inside Shoreline Excursions, armed and brandishing."

"Sheriff, I'm on my way." Surprisingly, it was Locke who responded first. "I'm less than a minute out."

"Park at the end of the street and block traffic before

approaching, Locke. Lettinger is working her way around to the back of the building."

"Addison. What the *hell* are you doing with that gun? Put it down before someone gets hurt." Cole Fairbank's muffled instructions carried through the large glass window at the front of his office.

Rebecca cursed under her breath. Keying her radio, she shared the update. "She's got Cole in there."

"Is he also a suspect?" Locke again.

"Affirmative." Rebecca hoped she was wrong. But also hoped she was right. If Cole was in on this, there were two people inside who needed to be taken down. If he wasn't, then this could turn nasty fast if he tried to stop his wife. Addison had already shown what she did to people who got in her way.

Staying low, Rebecca moved to the entrance. Keeping as much of her body shielded by the wall as possible, she grabbed the handle and pushed the door open.

"Stay out, Sheriff. I don't want to do anything we'll all regret later." Addison's voice was high-pitched and manic.

"You know I can't do that, Addison. I'm an officer of the law. I have to uphold that law." Using her words as a distraction, she twisted around and stood at the same time so she could peer inside.

Addison was at the other end of the small room, behind a desk, with her confused husband standing in the middle of the space. He caught sight of Rebecca and slowly raised his hands. His wife ducked behind his broad chest, using him as a shield. Rebecca seized the opportunity while Addison was on the move to dart inside the office and take cover next to a bookcase. From there, Addison had no shot.

The woman's gun was swaying wildly. First it pointed toward the bookcase where Rebecca was, then it swung in the direction of her own temple, and then, practically in slow motion, it came to rest against the side of Cole's head.

"Addy, what are you doing? What the hell is going on here?" Cole's voice shook, and he tried to move away.

"Don't move, Cole. I mean it." The steel barrel pressed harder against his temple.

"Come on, Addison. You don't want to do this. Kill your own husband? The man who loves you?"

Rebecca shifted slightly and got a better angle on Addison. They locked eyes.

"I love him. Truly. He was my first love, so I always will."

She started crying, and Rebecca knew this wasn't going anywhere good. Addison Fairbank was in a very dark place.

"But I was never his first love…"

"Yes, you were. Are. Yes, you are, honey. I love—"

"Shut up!" she shrieked. "First there was his mother, who always needs him by her side. Then there was the ocean. It's true what they say, a fisherman's true love is always the sea. And then there were his boats. Which he doted on. Doted on! They were his mistresses."

Through his terror, Cole seemed genuinely confused. "That's not fair. You can't compare my love for you to a—"

"I said shut the hell up! Liar! You're a liar!"

She choked on her words and her tears, and when she fixed her eyes on Rebecca again, they were filled with hesitancy, not hate.

"I'd be waiting for him at home, you know, but he wouldn't leave them until he'd cleaned every little nook and even polished all their brass." The woman wildly searched the room before she squeaked out her proclamation. "Don't pressure me, Sheriff. You don't know what I'm capable of."

Rebecca nodded, not sure if Addison could even see the agreement. But she needed to keep Addison's entire focus on her, that much she knew. Any minute now, Rhonda should be reaching the back door to prevent an escape.

"I do know what you're capable of, Addison. Maybe you didn't hear, but I was there when the boats were burning. And I know you're the one who did that. You probably didn't mean to kill Bolivar MacDaniel, but once you got started, you couldn't stop, right?"

"Right." Addison's hand started to shake, and the barrel of her gun danced along her husband's temple. "It was an accident."

Through the large front window out of her periphery, Rebecca spotted Locke running up the sidewalk to provide additional backup.

Cole swallowed hard. "That was Mac on the boat? He was a good man, Addy. What did you do?"

Addison ignored his words. "He was in the wrong place at the wrong time. Sometimes bad things happen to good people. I did what I had to do."

"Like with Oswald Chapman?"

A distressed whimper crept up Cole's throat. "Chapman? What?" His hands were still raised, and he looked terrified, but he seemed to be fighting the urge to turn on his wife.

"I don't know what you're talking about, Sheriff." Addison shook her head.

"Chapman was shot from close range, right in his chest. He's out of surgery. He survived his attempted murder."

"What? What are you saying? And why do we care about Oswald Chapman?" The barrel of her gun was knocking into her husband's head, she was shaking so visibly.

"Your boats, Chapman's and yours, both burned down, so I thought you'd want to know. And I'm certain he saw his assailant and would be more than happy to tell us who did it when he can. And I bet he'll even tell us why."

Locke slid next to the open door, his gun out and ready. He was only waiting for her cue to jump into action.

"He's a liar! He'll say anything just to make you believe him. He promised to loan me money to start my own business. But he didn't give me time before he started demanding I repay him."

"That's the problem when you sign a deal with the devil. You never know when he'll call that debt due." A sudden sucking breeze through the front door told Rebecca that Rhonda had opened the back door. Rebecca peered around the bookcase to find Rhonda's gaze fixed on Addison, her gun aimed at the woman's head.

So far, Addison hadn't noticed. "My back was against the wall. The loan's interest rate was so high I couldn't make the payments. When he suggested burning the boat for the insurance money, I couldn't afford to say no."

"What?" Cole whimpered.

"I knew the insurance money would be enough to pay Oswald back and still replace the boat and equipment. I had it all under control. Until Mac showed up on the boat and tried to be a hero and put out the fire."

"When you said you would do anything to get your stupid marketing business to turn a profit, I never thought you'd be willing to kill!" Cole, in a moment of righteous anger or extreme stupidity, started to turn on his wife, his arms dropping threateningly.

"No!" Rebecca yelled to stop his fatal mistake and cover any possible sounds as Rhonda crept up behind Addison.

"Oswald didn't think I would do it either." His wife's ice-cold voice froze Cole in place. "I did all of this to prove to you how serious I was about forging my own way in this world. Don't make it be the last thing you learn in this life. I will destroy you much easier than I did your boat. And we all know I'm not going to stop just because someone gets in my way."

Before Cole pushed his luck, Rhonda's arm came up under Addison's gun arm, sweeping it high and to the side.

"Get off me!" the manic woman screamed.

Rebecca raced forward, Locke at her back.

Rhonda's fingers slipped into Addison's palm and shoved the gun out of her grip.

Cole jerked, and Rebecca grabbed him by the collar, yanking him out of the way.

Locke trained his gun on Addison as her eyes went wide, and Rhonda grabbed her arms from behind and rode her to the ground, knocking the wind out of her.

"Don't worry, Addison, we'll make sure everyone knows how far you were willing to go for money," Rhonda huffed in the young woman's ear.

Rebecca knelt beside the special agent. "Addison Fairbank, you're under arrest for arson, murder, attempted murder, and insurance fraud."

43

Rebecca walked past Viviane to refill her coffee cup as her deputy followed her, assaulting her with questions. "All of this because she signed a shitty loan contract?"

It had been a long and exhausting day. Collecting evidence from three different crime scenes at the same time had used every piece of tech they had on the books. Most of the damning proof had been carried out of Oswald Chapman's home office in sealed boxes.

Everything there would be reviewed with a fine-tooth comb as the county, state, and federal agencies all had charges to file against the man.

"Yep. Once she was on the hook with him, she felt like she had to do whatever he asked. All her hopes and dreams were wrapped up in that money he'd loaned her." Rebecca took a little breather, leaning against the table, and finished the last few gulps of her cold coffee.

"Good thing I found copies of those loan documents at his house." Hoyt smiled but was so tired all it did was add to the wrinkles under his eyes, deepening his haggard appearance.

"It was. Great job on that." Rebecca tilted her mug at him in a lame cheers motion before refilling it. "If you hadn't, then she might have had the time to dispose of the rest of the evidence. As is, she's singing like a canary, just hoping to take him down with her. Turns out, Chapman had needed to destroy any evidence that might be on his boat before the Feds could get their hands on it."

"Why didn't he just sail it into the middle of the ocean and sink it?" Locke was the only one of them who didn't look like he'd been put through the wringer. Then again, he was used to working the night shift.

"Greed will get you every time." Hoyt let out a loud groan as he stood up. "Ah, jeez, standing all day is getting harder every year. That dumbass wanted the insurance money he would get for his boat. He probably planned to sue Cole because that's where the fire originated."

"He's a millionaire. And now he's going to prison for the rest of his life as an accessory to all of Addison's crimes because he wanted his one-hundred-and-seventy-thousand-dollar payout." Viviane shook her head.

"And the Feds managed to get warrants on his other offices because of his arrest and Addison's confession." Rebecca pushed away from the table to head back to her desk.

Reaching the edge of the bullpen, she caught movement through the front windows of the station. Richmond Vale slung the front door open and, as soon as he saw her, started to shake his finger. "All you had to do was solve a simple arson crime, and you failed to do that! Now Oswald is in the hospital? Why can't you do anything right?"

His yelling didn't cover the sound of three sets of feet hitting the floor as her deputies swarmed behind her.

"All of you! Why are you here when there are crimes to

be solved? Get back out there and find out who shot my friend, or I'll make sure you all lose your jobs!"

Rebecca blinked at him over the rim of her steaming mug. "Already done."

Vale spluttered to a halt. "What? What did you say?"

"I said done. We caught the person who shot Chapman. And we caught the people responsible for the boat fires. The crime scenes are being watched while evidence is being collected. And don't worry, your buddy Oswald will get government-grade medical care while he awaits his trial for those fires."

Locke nudged her shoulder. "And the felony murder charge."

"Oh, that's right! And the felony murder charge." She nodded. "See, my people have everything under control. You don't need to worry about anything. We've got this."

"What do you mean, murder charge?" Vale's face went white as he stared at Rebecca.

She smiled and took two steps closer to him. "I mean he's under arrest, awaiting arraignment, while handcuffed to his hospital bed with guards posted outside his door. And instead of worrying about me doing my job, maybe you should be worrying about what kind of stories Chapman might tell the authorities in exchange for a reduced sentence. After all, the man earns his living by making deals that benefit him."

Dick spluttered a few more syllables before turning and stomping out the door as fast as he'd entered.

"Ahh, that was just what I needed to end this day on a good note." Rebecca turned to face her team. "Frost, Darby, it's after nine. Go home. You've done a great job tonight. But I still expect you to be on time for your shifts in the morning."

Hoyt, not needing to be told twice, immediately headed for the front door. "You remember that when nine a.m. rolls around, Boss. Can't have the sheriff showing up late. Otherwise, people'll talk about how you're not doing your job."

Rebecca laughed without mirth and headed toward her office. "You talk as if I'm going to have time to go home tonight, Frost. There's still the FBI and staties to deal with. And Rhonda's not done with her investigation either."

44

Rebecca was seated in her office finishing up some miscellaneous reports. The last week had been a mountain of paperwork.

Chapman had regained consciousness a few days after being shot, realized his predicament, and begun screaming about suing. Apparently, being handcuffed to a hospital bed didn't sit well with the man. His protestations of innocence had been loud enough to wake the dead. Then last night, he'd taken a turn for the worse. She was waiting to hear news of his condition.

Rhonda appeared in her doorway. "I'm done with my investigation."

"About time. Does that mean I get my office back to myself?" Rebecca pointed to the coffee table that was still sitting where Rhonda had left it.

She laughed and leaned against the doorframe. "Hey, if you didn't want extra guests in here, then you shouldn't have gotten such cozy chairs. It's a lot easier to work in here than it is in the lounge. Besides, we rarely get to socialize outside of work, so I take what I can get."

That made Rebecca smile. Benji, her old partner from the Bureau, had said the same thing last time he'd come down to visit and had followed her around town while she worked a case. "Next thing you know, you'll be accusing me of being a workaholic."

"I don't know about that. I'm not one for making wild accusations like that without proof." Rhonda grinned at her and casually leaned over to stare at the toiletry bag Rebecca hadn't yet stowed after her shower. "Which I have you to thank for. I went way too hard after Serenity. If you hadn't knocked some sense into me, we would've been chasing a dead-end lead while the real suspect fled."

"High prey drive. I totally get it. Happens in a lot of people."

Rhonda gave her a considering smile. "I think you just compared me to a dog."

Rebecca shrugged noncommittally. "Maybe, but I like dogs more than I like most people, so take it as a compliment."

"Then I'll take it in the spirit it was intended." Rhonda arched her back, stretching her muscles. "But seriously, I feel the need to apologize. I was overzealous in my efforts to appear neutral in my investigation. From what I've seen, you and your people operate at the highest level of integrity. It's remarkable, really. Accept my apology?"

"Of course. I understand you were doing your job. I think you could have gone about it differently, but in the end, we're both on the same side. And that's what matters."

Rhonda grinned, the sincerity of it reaching her eyes. "Walk me out?"

Rebecca stood. "Sure. Did you just stop in to say goodbye, then?"

"I was also going to put your furniture back where I got

it from, but once you mentioned it, I decided not to." Rhonda laughed. "Besides, with the way things have been going and the way I think they'll keep going, you might want to keep that table in there for the next messy case that lands on your desk."

"Every case involving the Yacht Club is messy. But thanks for jinxing us." They stepped into the bullpen and Rebecca waited while Rhonda took a moment to wave goodbye to Hoyt, Viviane, and Jake. "But recently, everything seems to connect back to the Yacht Club. I swear they have more layers than an onion, which is why I always do my due diligence with each case. You never know which one's going to end up leading right back to those rich assholes."

"It does seem that way. But you keep doing what you're doing, and I think you're going to be okay." Rhonda gave her a knowing smile. "At least, that's what my investigation proved. I'll be keeping an eye on things on my end. Make sure to call if you need anything. I've got your back."

That was such a relief to hear, Rebecca nearly hugged the special agent. But instead, she settled for a hearty handshake and a curt nod.

The phone rang, and Elliot picked it up with a cheerful greeting.

It was good to know that not only could she trust her staff, she could also trust her gut. Her instincts had said Rhonda was someone she could rely on, and even last week's issues hadn't changed that.

"Sheriff West?"

Rebecca glanced over at Elliot, lifting her cup to her lips. "Hmm?"

"The Sandpiper Bank has triggered its silent alarm."

The End
To be continued...

Thank you for reading.
All of the *Shadow Island Series* books can be found on Amazon.

ACKNOWLEDGMENTS

How does one properly thank everyone involved in taking a dream and making it a reality? Here goes.

In addition to our families, whose unending support provided the foundation for us to find the time and energy to put these thoughts on paper, we want to thank the editors who polished our words and made them shine.

Many thanks to our publisher for risking taking on two newbies and giving us the confidence to become bona fide authors.

More than anyone, we want to thank you, our readers, for sharing your most important asset, your time, with this book. We hope with all our hearts we made it worthwhile.

Much love,
Mary & Lori

ABOUT THE AUTHOR

Mary Stone lives among the majestic Blue Ridge Mountains of East Tennessee with her two dogs, four cats, a couple of energetic boys, and a very patient husband.

As a young girl, she would go to bed every night, wondering what type of creature might be lurking underneath. It wasn't until she was older that she learned that the creatures she needed to most fear were human.

Today, she creates vivid stories with courageous, strong heroines and dastardly villains. She invites you to enter her world of serial killers, FBI agents but never damsels in distress. Her female characters can handle themselves, going toe-to-toe with any male character, protagonist or antagonist.

Discover more about Mary Stone on her website.
www.authormarystone.com

Lori Rhodes

As a tiny girl, from the moment Lori Rhodes first dipped her toe into the surf on a barrier island of Virginia, she was in love. When she grew up and learned all the deep, dark secrets and horrible acts people could commit against each other, she couldn't stop the stories from coming out of the other end of her pen. Somehow, her magical island and the darkness got mixed together and ended up in her first novel.

Now, she spends her days making sure the guests at her beach rental cottages are happy, and her nights dreaming up the characters who love her island as much as she does.

Connect with Mary Online

facebook.com/authormarystone
x.com/MaryStoneAuthor
goodreads.com/AuthorMaryStone
bookbub.com/profile/3378576590
pinterest.com/MaryStoneAuthor
instagram.com/marystoneauthor
tiktok.com/@authormarystone

Made in the USA
Middletown, DE
21 November 2024